The "BE-BOP-A-LULA" Kid

Bruce Brinkley

For my wife, Audrey,

*Mother of the coolest
two men I know.*

*And for Ryan and Griffith,
sons of the coolest wife ever.*

ACKNOWLEDGEMENTS

Some of the ideas in this story were inspired by my sons' experiences. I'm thankful for the times we had together when they were younger. Thanks to Griff, the musician, and to Ryan, the artist.

Thanks to my uncle Jim Harcum for introducing me to the world of rock 'n' roll. Thanks to my good friend Jack Neal, Gene Vincent's original bass player. I'm grateful to Jack and his wife Betty for sharing many stories about their experiences with the Blue Caps.

Thanks to Theresa Oliveto, Catherine Heartwell, Soraia Brinkley, Norman Cohn, and Amy Simmons for reading my manuscript, suggesting changes, and for expressing their insight.

Thanks to my Cape Charles neighbors, Dianna and Tony Curtis and their children, Kyle, Reiley, and Carly. Your enthusiasm and editorial suggestions are greatly appreciated.

Special thanks to Kristin Lewis, my friend and thirteen-year-old editor. Thanks for correcting my grammar and spelling and syntax. Thanks for making my dialogue sound "…more like Cape Charles." Thanks for the notes written across the pages of my manuscript. You turned it into a work of art.

Thanks to Audrey for listening, for all of the re-readings, your patience with me, and for your undying love. Thanks for your encouragement and faith in me.

Trash Dump

The Great
Chesapeake
Bay

Beach

Jefferson Avenue

Madison Avenue

The
Pavilion

Cape Charles, Virginia

august 22, 1956
Llewellyn "Whitual
"Zhater"

Mason Avenue

North

Washington Avenue

To King Creek

Plum Street

Madison Street

Fig Street

Cape Charles School

Gill's Home

Ball Field

Bennett Avenue

Monroe Avenue

My House

Peach Street

Tazewell Avenue

St. Charles Church

Fitch Street

Fire House

Old Ice Plant

To:
The Railroad Shops
The Gypsy Camp
Route 23

INTRODUCTION

The orange sun burst over the tree tops that separated the tiny town of Cape Charles from the Atlantic Ocean. On the morning after seeing their first live rock 'n' roll show, thirteen-year-old Skeeter yanked the pillow off his head, rolled onto his back, and stared at his bedroom ceiling. Usually, the last day of summer vacation was spent trying to squeeze the most fun possible into the few hours before bed time. But for Skeeter, this last day of summer marked the beginning of a new life. This morning he awoke not as a boy, but as a teenager, a real teenager, something he had wanted to be since the first day he'd heard the song.

Across town, Jill, the same age as Skeeter, washed the breakfast dishes, put the bacon and butter back into the refrigerator, and wiped off the kitchen table. Finally, her father and brothers had stopped their questions about the night before, and her first "date."

"It wasn't a date," she raised her voice in response. "You know we're best friends."

Jill knew she had to get ready for her first day of class in a new school and in a new town. That was of no concern to her and she could handle herself. Now alone, she flopped down backwards on her army cot of a bed and studied the cracks in the ceiling of the run down house her father had rented. This morning, Jill was sure of only two things. She would never again be the tomboy she had been all her life. And, she didn't want to see Skeeter that day.

Introduction

My name is Rueben. I'm a crow. That's right, and, a rather large crow at that. I don't know exactly how old I am because it's of no concern to me. Skeeter could probably tell you because humans keep up with that sort of thing. Crows don't.

You don't mind if I call you Bud, do you? Good. Now, as the most wonderful summer of my life ends and the harsh cold of winter approaches, I now have the time to relay a story to you. That's right, to you, Bud.

It is a story about a boy and a girl, simple as that. You, my friend, may decide about whom. I've watched them all summer. I've flown above them as they moved about town and sailed overhead as they skimmed along the waters of the Chesapeake Bay. I've perched on their heads and shoulders. I've shared their meals and their most precious secrets. This story is my gift to you.

September 1, 1956

Rueben
An American Crow

CHAPTER I

"Strike him out! Strike him out!" Skeeter smiled at the chants from his classmates.

"Get a hit, Skeeter! Hit a long one, Skeet," his team mates yelled.

The last day of sixth grade and Skeeter had taken his final test. The salt air of the nearby Atlantic Ocean filled his nose and lifted his spirits with the excitement of being free like only a summer kid could be. He just got his summer haircut, a crew cut, same as always. He could wear short pants and no shoes all summer.

Since there was no written test for Physical Education class, the teacher gathered the kids together after lunch for a game of softball to fill the last period of the final day of the school year.

Skeeter stood in the batter's box and stretched his bat across the plate. His white high top Converse All Stars balanced his thin frame as he leaned in front of the catcher. What could be better, he thought and stared at his friend, Junior, winding up the pitch. Junior's arm swung backward, stopped for an instant and moved in Skeeter's direction. As the ball arched upward and then toward him, Skeeter shifted his weight to his back leg and swung with all his might.

"Smack!" The sound of the ball hitting the wooden bat was a sweet thing to Skeeter's ears. The ball went so high that Skeeter lost it in the sun. The center fielder and the short stop couldn't see it either. Skeeter ran hard to first base. The ball was still in the air. He touched the cloth sack they used for a base and headed for second. He knew if someone caught the fly ball he would be out. As the ball spun to the ground each kid thought some other kid would catch it.

Whomp! The ball hit the concrete-hard dirt with the same power that sent it skyward seconds before. Wenus scooped it up and tossed it underhand to the second baseman. Skeeter was flying. Before he could execute his best slide, Eddy, the second baseman, caught the toss, and stepped right in front of Skeeter. And since Skeeter was running about a hundred miles an hour, there was no way he could avoid running into Eddy.

They all heard the snap of Skeeter's forearm when it broke as the two boys collided. It was a sickening sound that made you hurt inside. Skeeter landed face down in the gray dirt. He held his broken arm to his chest and protected it from the fall with his right. He felt his breath burst out of his lungs as he hit the ground. Skeeter's friends heard his moans and each watched in amazement.

From my favorite limb in a huge oak, my heart raced as I watched Skeeter squeeze his eyes shut to help block out the pain in his arm. I leapt off the branch, spread my big black wings and glided to the ground near my friend.

"Skeet. Skeet." Many of them called out.

"Go get a teacher." Some ordered to no one in particular.

Some girl yelled, "Go get his mom."

"Get his dad." Another kid said.

"Get the priest. Get Father Ryan."

The boys rolled Skeeter face up. The few girls who were nearby kept their distance, huddled together, and squeezed their books to their chests. The dust around Skeeter's forehead and on his neck mixed with sweat and turned to mud.

Once the salt air filled his lungs again, he felt a little better. Skeeter couldn't believe how badly his arm hurt. He looked down at it. Under his skin his arm bone was now twisted and no longer in a straight line. It hurt worse when he looked at it.

Junior knelt beside him. "You're gonna' be OK, Skeet."

"Yea, you'll get fixed up fine." Wenus told him.

Skeeter sat still while Coach Higgins looked at it. "Just stay here a while, son. Your dad's on his way."

Shadrack crossed the grassy outfield from the cafeteria and handed Skeeter a glass of water.

"Thanks," Skeeter said, gulping the cool drink and feeling it run out the corners of his mouth. He cradled his arm as if it were a new puppy.

In all the confusion and even with my deep concern for Skeeter, my attention was drawn, like a tack to a magnet, toward a black pickup truck that crawled past the ball field. Packing boxes peeked out from beneath a canvas cover, tattered from hundreds of miles of highway driving. Black and gray smoke coughed out of the tailpipe. And by the time I noticed the truck, I couldn't see the faces of the occupants. Two young men in a beat-up sedan followed close behind. I had never seen either vehicle in Cape Charles before and I didn't know then the cause of my curious attraction.

"Does it hurt?" Peanut was in a trance staring at the twisted arm.

"Yea, it hurts." Skeeter snapped back.

"Sorry, that was a stupid question."

Skeeter didn't say anything else. His arm throbbed now, sort of like a little marching man inside his arm beating on a bass drum. He began to feel sick, too.

"Come on son, I'll walk you home. Can you walk OK?" Coach asked.

"Yes sir, I can walk."

The coach motioned to the others. "You boys pick up the baseball gear and report back to the classroom. It's almost time for the bell to ring."

The coach knew when a kid got hurt, there was a short period of time when kids behaved like they should. It was as if all kids have unwritten and unspoken rules of a brotherhood. It was probably out of respect for the hurt kid.

From the park in front of the school, Skeeter could hardly focus on the two blocks to Fig Street where Monroe Avenue crossed. He and the coach didn't talk anymore. They crossed Nectarine and continued east. I flew circles overhead. I felt weak seeing my best friend in so much pain.

We all heard the familiar sound of the '55 Chevy turning onto Monroe. Timing was perfect and we all got to Skeeter's house at the same time.

"Havin' bad luck on the last day of school, Skeeter?" His dad could always make him feel better by acting like nothing was as serious as it seemed.

"Yes sir. Does my arm look broke?"

"It looks pretty crooked to me," his dad answered. "What do you think Coach?"

"I'd bet money on it, Sir."

Skeeter wondered how long it would take before his mother would come running out of the house in hysterics. He hated when she made a big ruckus over him. It was embarrassing.

Skeeter's dad shook the coach's hand. "Thanks for looking after my boy. I suppose we need to wash up and head across the bay to see a bone doctor."

"No problem, Sir. Glad to do it. Skeeter, you take care now. I just might come by tomorrow and see how you're doin.'"

"Thanks," Skeeter said. "I'll be OK"

Skeeter's mom burst through the front door, ran toward him, and threw her arms around his neck. "How's my baby? How bad is it?"

Chapter 1

"Be careful Mom." He raised his lifeless arm as high as he could without it hurting worse. "Just don't look at it."

"Why Baby? Let me see." Before Skeeter could turn his arm away from her, she stood up and stared at the twisted limb.

"Mom, don't look."

Skeeter watched the color drain from his mother's face. She collapsed to her knees. "Dear God!"

"Now Mother, calm down." Skeeter heard his father trying to console her. He never understood why parents called each other Mother and Father in front of their kids, like they were kids too. It was confusing. Kind of stupid, too.

His father took charge. "It's a rite of passage for every boy to break a bone. That's part of becoming a man. He'll be alright. I know you're scared to death, but throwin' a conniption fit here in the front yard isn't helpin' anybody feel better, especially Skeeter. Now we have to get goin' if we're gonna catch the ferry to Norfolk."

I saw the tears running down his mother's cheeks. She was white as grits and I felt a little sorry for her. Skeeter's father had calmed her down, but she continued to sniffle.

"I'll pack you two a snack for the trip." Skeeter's mom sniffed.

"Thanks, Mom. Mom?"

"What, Honey?" She honked her nose into her hanky.

"I'll be OK. Please don't worry. And will you please stop carryin' on over me? It's embarrassin'."

"Now Skeeter, you know that every mother crow think's her baby is the blackest."

"Yes Ma'am."

Skeeter and I have heard that saying a million times. I'm the one who should know about mother crows. I am a crow, remember?

CHAPTER 2

I wasn't able to stow away on the S.S. Pocahontas, the ferry that took Skeeter and his father across the bay to Norfolk. I heard the story of the trip many times as he told each of his friends in the weeks that followed. The two-hour ferry ride seemed longer than usual and the pain in Skeeter's arm got worse as the time went by. The doctor's office was located in a tall medical office building in the city and the smell of alcohol drenched the waiting room. Skeeter felt sick in his stomach when the doctor first grabbed his arm.

After an X-ray or two and several shots of pain killer in Skeeter's arm, he sat on an examination table and wondered what would happen next. Skeeter's dad and the doctor exchanged casual conversation and Skeeter managed to relax a little. But then, and without an explanation or warning, the doctor grabbed Skeeter's arm, placed one hand on each side of the broken bone, and with a torturing sound of bones crunching, twisted Skeeter's arm until he felt it snap back into place. Skeeter told about his experience many times and it continues to make me weak when I think of it.

Skeeter stood in front of a full length mirror in the examining room and saw the reflection of the 5'5" boy he expected to see. He saw a face that was blood drained from the shock of the doctor wrenching his arm back into position. His blue eyes had been replaced with bloodshot looking ping pong balls. A hard white cast covered his left arm from his elbow to his knuckles.

Chapter 2

"Now, don't get that cast wet, Son," the doctor said. "Or, you'll be back over here to get a new one."

There was a drug store in the lobby of the building and Skeeter's dad led him through the thick glass door.

"How about a milkshake, Skeeter? I think that would make us both feel better."

"Really? Yes sir. That would be great."

Skeeter sipped the frozen delight and spun back and forth on the lunch counter stool.

"What are those books for, Dad?'"

"They're diaries. Look, some have locks with keys so you can keep what you write secret. No one should read another person's personal diary without permission, you know. Pick one out, if you want and you can record everything you do during your first year as a teenager."

Later, on the ferry ride back to Cape Charles, Skeeter recorded the first entry in his new diary: June 8, 1956. I broke my arm today. The summer has to get better.

I waited for their return for hours at the ferry terminal in Kiptopeke and flew in circles around the car as it rolled down the ramp. I flew a short cut across the coast to be there when they got home.

"Wake up, Son. We're home." His dad said, tapping on the cast.

"Cack, Cack, Cack." I was happy to see them.

"Hey, Rue." Skeeter said. "I don't feel so good."

Once home and from the roof of the front porch, I saw Skeeter drag himself up the stairs from the kitchen and turn right at the landing. Then holding his cast with his right arm, he slid along the walls of the hallway to his room. He climbed onto his bed and within a few seconds, was well into dream land. I settled into a comfortable spot near his window and waited for morning.

The sun had been shining through his window for an hour before he got up. Skeeter grabbed his cast as soon as he was conscious. It was still there. He hoped that this had been a dream and that he'd wake up without a broken arm. He didn't want to be prisoner to a cast all summer. Am I still dreamin'? He wondered.

He remembered slugging up the stairs from the kitchen, making the right turn on the landing as he'd done ten million times before. He remembered falling across his bed and remembered nothing after that.

How he came to be standing in his room, staring at the spinning record player and wiping drool from his slippery chin, he had no recollection. With glazed and watery eyes his other four senses had lost connection with his brain. All Skeeter knew was that the music he was hearing must surely be the righteous fluting of the pied piper himself. Over and over the arm of his red and white record player drifted off the last groove, slid across the paper label of the record, hiccupped, and reached out to the edge again. At 45 revolutions per minute, Skeeter sensed he had been reborn.

Yes, a Baptism. It must be a true epiphany. Never had Skeeter, or many other people, in Cape Charles, ever experienced this sound.

Chapter 2

"What is this? Who is this?" Skeeter mumbled through the spit stringing from his chin.

Skeeter's hand instinctively reached for the volume control and spun it to 10, the loudest setting on the dial. Forty-five times, over and over, the greatest song to be born in the lifetime of Llewellyn "Skeeter" Whitmel, spun him delirious.

"Be-bop-a-lula, she's my baby, be-bop-a-lula, I don't mean maybe." The singer sang over and over. The guy singing the words was like nothing he'd ever heard. Skeeter learned by heart, the words, and the music too, in only a few minutes. If kids could learn school studies as fast as Skeeter learned this, kids would all be geniuses.

When I heard it, I too began to twitch and stomp around uncontrollably. I was a crow gone mad. Trying to tap both feet at the same time, Skeeter had to steady himself with his desk chair. He felt an uncontrollable urge to dance. The bones shaking inside his pants legs looked like two punching bags full of flopping fish. His arms were swinging like a fat lady shooing flies off a blue ribbon pie at the Fourth of July Picnic. Skeeter buzzed around his room like a June bug freed from a Mason jar.

After about an hour and forty-five minutes, a big hand with the usual four fingers and a thumb moved up and down in front of Skeeter's face. Gradually coming out of his trance, Skeeter rotated his eyes, leaving his head aimed at the record player. His eyes followed along the arm that was connected to the waving hand and stopped on the face of his Uncle Jimmy.

"Hi, Jimmy." Skeeter stared at his uncle.

"I guess you like this song. I knew you would," he said. "Listen to this. 'BE-BOP-A-LULA' is part of a new kind of music called rock 'n' roll. Sometimes you can hear it on the radio but mostly you have to go to a record store to hear it."

Skeeter knew that the few radio stations broadcast to the Eastern Shore would never play this stuff.

"The guy singing the song is Gene Vincent and he's lived in Norfolk, Princess Anne County, and in Portsmouth, all around. The band is called "The Blue Caps" and they are from the local area too. I brought this record for you."

"Wow. Thanks." Skeeter hugged his uncle.

I once heard Skeeter tell Wenus that his Uncle Jimmy was ten years older than Skeeter, and knew everything. "He graduated from high school, had a cool job, and a sweet car, a '56 Buick Special, that he bought with his own money."

Actually, his cool job was working at the coal piers in Norfolk where he got covered in coal dust everyday. But to Skeeter, it sure beat going to Cape Charles School.

I want to tell you something now, Bud. You must be careful about what you do, when you think you're alone. Well, here's a good one for just you and me. It cracks me up. I really don't mean to betray a friend, but sometimes you just have to have a little fun with one.

After Uncle Jimmy left for Norfolk, Skeeter went up to his room and played "BE-BOP-A-LULA" a thousand more times. With the record playing, he dances around his room doing the jitterbug or some strange dance and looks like he has bloomer crickets. And, to this day whenever he gets so mentally involved with Gene Vincent, and he thinks no one can see him, he does the same dance. He waves his arms around in a half stiff motion pretending he is playing some invisible guitar. He weaves around a make-believe stage singing to the crowd. Occasionally, he winks at the air. I don't understand that because he's given no hint of having interest in girls looking at him. During the attacks, he is quite ridiculous looking, but extremely amusing.

I just thought of something funny, Bud. Want to play a game with me? Now, I've just described my good friend Skeeter imitating his idol. Suppose we call this delirium a "GENE ATTACK." Got it? From now on, when I shout out, "GENE ATTACK," come back here and read it because Skeeter is doing it again. Or, if you're really good at imagining, you can commit this to memory. Ha. Ha. Ha. How clever of us.

CHAPTER 3

Skeeter liked to walk the alleys of Cape Charles and poke around inside of empty buildings. And, after he broke his arm, he spent a lot of time kicking around town. One day just before dusk, he ventured behind the brick buildings on Mason Avenue. Reaching the rear of the smaller building he saw what appeared to be a boy about his size facing away from him. Skeeter's foot brushed against a garbage can lid and the kid turned around quickly. Skeeter saw smoke rising from the boy's hand. It wasn't a boy, but a waif of a girl standing there, holding a cigarette. She lifted her hand up and put the cigarette to her lips. She squinted and sucked some smoke out of it and into her mouth. She exhaled real fast staring at Skeeter the whole time. I could tell she wanted to cough but held it in for Skeeter's sake.

She had brown hair with a hint of red. Cut short, it would be hard to know from a distance if she were a boy or a girl. Her fingers were long and thin with ragged nails at their tips. She wasn't dirty, but she wasn't clean looking either.

"What you lookin' at?" The girl said, the smoke muffling her words. "Git outta' here!" she ordered.

Skeeter just stood for a minute looking at her. Her clothes looked like hand-me-downs (or as Skeeter would say, "handy downs") from an older brother. Her shoes matched the rest of her, kinda scruffy. They were boys' shoes, actually, just like Skeeter's.

"Put that thing out." Skeeter said. He pointed at the cigarette.

The girl glared back. "You think you can make me? You're not the boss of me."

"I don't really care what you do." Skeeter told her.

They stood still each waiting for the other to say something. The girl took another puff then dropped the cigarette on the cinder driveway and mashed it to death.

"You smoke much?" She asked him.

"Not much. I mean I never tried smoking and I never want to."

The girl looked at Skeeter's arm. "What happened to your wing?"

"What wing?"

"Your arm, Goof." She acted very cocky.

"It got broke."

"I can see that. How'd you break it?"

"Playin' baseball. And, on the last day of school, too."

"You always have bad luck?"

"Last school year I did."

She pointed her finger at him, "Don't let it rub off on me."

"Where'd you get it?" Skeeter asked her.

"Get what?"

"The cigarette." He was beginning to dislike her.

"Over at the park. A man got off the park bench in a hurry and left his empty pack. But, I noticed, after I figured he wasn't comin' back, that there was one Pall Mall inside.

Later, I found some matches. I thought I was hidin' good until you got here." She stared at Skeeter a minute or so. "Well, I'd better git." She aimed herself toward the street and stomped right past Skeeter. Just before she got to the end of the alley, she took off running and turned at the corner of the building. It was as if she were trying to get a head start in a race or something.

She called me a 'goof,' he thought to himself. What's with that?

"Smokin.'" He heard himself say. "What a jerk."

The girl ran hard and fast, north on Pine, then east on Tazewell. When she got to Peach Street she looked back to see if anyone had noticed her.

I took off too. I tried to blend in with the ordinary looking birds in town. You know, I'm much better looking than most, Bud. There's no need to look suspicious. Even though I was curious about this tomboy, I didn't want to spook her.

I watched her walk toward a gray weathered two story house, the last house on Peach, next to the park. I took a position in the back yard where I could see into the well-lit kitchen.

"Where you been, Baby?" A tall, thin, man with brick red hair pushed at some fish sizzling in a black iron skillet. I could smell the grease of the operation and the thought of fresh fish made me realize how hungry I was.

"Daddy, why'd we have to rent a house on *Peach* Street. It sounds like a street for girls. *Peach* Street. I hate

Peach Street. It's hardly a street. Two and a half blocks long is hardly a street anyway."

"Whoa, mule. Hold on here now. What you got a bee in your bonnet about?" The man's voice was strong and clear. It wasn't a big man's gruff voice. It was mellow and comforting. It was smooth and calming despite the cigarette smoke he inhaled every minute or so.

"Hey, Jill." A young man with the same color hair as the father had come down the stairs. He had straight white teeth that sparkled when he grinned. His freckled skin was similar to Jill's and it made me think immediately that he was her brother. He looked about twenty or so. "How's my favorite little sister?"

I was right. He was her brother. I'm too smart for my own good.

Posing like a boxer, he held up his fists and asked Jill, "You kick any Cape Charles butt, yet?"

"No. But, I'll kick yours anytime I feel like it."

The boy laughed and said, "Hold on there Annie Oakley. I said Cape Charles butt. I know you can kick Lee County butt. Hey Pop," the brother said, "I met some guys at work who play poker on Tuesday nights. They told me to bring you along too. Wanna' go?"

"Jill. Dump those potatoes in the sink and get out the butter, please." Pop said. "Where's the card game? I'd like to go but I don't want to leave your sister."

Jill spilled the little red potatoes into the sink, dried them with kitchen towels, and put them in a bowl. With one of the sharp knives, she cut several slices across each of them and layered small chunks of butter on top. She watched the butter melt into the slice marks, over the skins, and then puddle in the bottom of the bowl.

"Crap." Jill spun around then ran onto the side porch. She returned with a handful of leaves. She held them under the tap giving them a good washing. She spread the small curly green leaves on a cutting board and blotted them until they were dry. With the smallest knife, she chopped the leaves into tiny pieces and sprinkled them onto the buttery potatoes.

"What cha' got there, Angel?" The dad asked.

"The neighbor lady gave me some parsley from her garden. I've been savin' it. Some day I might be a famous chef."

"Who's a famous chef?" Another boy appeared from the stairs. His hair was browner than his brother's, and he was chubby, maybe eighteen.

"I think I'll marry a famous chef," he said. "Then she can make a lot of money cookin' in some big city restaurant and come home and cook somethin' special for me every night of the week."

"Ha." the other brother said. "You'll be lucky to get any kinda' wife, Porky."

The father moved the fish from the skillet to a platter. "That's enough. Help Jill set the table. It's your turn to say grace, Baby."

The girl's family sat down at the kitchen table, held hands and waited for Jill to begin.

31

Chapter 3

Jill squeezed her eyes shut. "Lord, please bless this food you gave us. Please receive our prayers for it. Please bless our family. And Lord, please bless Momma and let her know we miss her and will always love her. Amen."

"Amen," they whispered, then finished their meal in silence.

CHAPTER 4

Since Jill and I had not been formally introduced, nor was she aware of my presence, I could easily gather data about her. OK. You caught me Bud. I couldn't help spying on her. Most of Skeeter's friends wouldn't be around this summer. With summer camps, family vacations, and extended stays with grandparents, Skeeter was destined to entertain himself. It was my wish that these two somehow get to know each other.

Jill and her family moved to Cape Charles the day school ended for the summer. She hadn't had an opportunity to meet any kids. I watched her wash the dishes, dry them, and finally put them in a cupboard. Her father and brothers left the house to have adventures of their own. Jill switched off the overhead light then disappeared from the kitchen. A different light switched on in the front of the house. I flew in the direction of the lighted room and lit in a beech tree at the south corner of the building.

This must be her room. She walked in my direction and for a second, I froze. How stupid. She couldn't see me in the dark while she was in the bright light of the room. Under the window were a small desk and an oddly built chair that didn't match. Jill sat down and pulled open the drawer under the center of the top. She took out a book and fumbled for a pencil.

"Dear Diary," Jill wrote the two words with a slow and precise motion. She poised her pencil to begin the next line. But, she just sat. She stared at the page. Nothing happened. Then, she popped out of the chair and scooted out of the room. I heard her fumbling around on the first floor. In a jiffy, she was back with a wooden box, the size of a loaf of bread. It had a brass lock built into the body of the box. She produced a brass key from her pants pocket and slipped it into the key slot. On the top was carved, J I L L, in block letters. Faded gold paint sat deep in each carved letter.

She fumbled with the contents for a few seconds. I heard leaves rustle in the tree above me and I cocked my head in that direction. I looked down Peach Street and over at the park next to Jill's house. It must have been the wind making the creepy noise and not someone spying on me.

When I looked toward Jill's window, she was again staring at her diary. But now, cigarette smoke curled around her head. She shaped the letter "O" with her lips and blew the smoke out of her mouth. The wind from the south drifted in her room and back out the east taking the smoke ring with it.

Oh, I wish she wouldn't do that.

Then, she must have gathered her thoughts. She wrote for several minutes without stopping. I watched the cigarette burn in a glass ashtray on her desk. I hoped it would burn out without her puffing it again.

Not lucky enough though. Jill glanced at it, picked up the now short butt and sucked as much smoke as she could without burning her finger tips.

She stubbed the fire end into the bottom of the dish. Pounding it until smoke no longer came off it, she put her fingertips to her mouth.

"Damn it. I hate smoking'."

Good. I thought. Then why don't you stop doing it?

Jill read out loud. "Dear Diary. I haven't met any kids since moving to this place, Cape Charles. I'm not sure I want to anyway. After my chores, I spent most of the day walking around town. Daddy brought fish home tonight and we had oysters and clams already, too. The lady next door gave me some parsley. I put it on the potatoes for supper. Daddy said it made them taste real special. I told them I wanted to be a famous chef one day. Maybe I will too. Maybe I can get a job in a café and get the cook to teach me things. Nobody would hire a girl anyway. Not a thirteen year old.

Before supper, I was sneaking a smoke behind some buildings. It was starting to get dark. Some goof ball boy caught me. He told me I shouldn't smoke. If he think's he's gonna tell me what to do, he's crazy. He acted all high and mighty and better than me. Well, not really, I guess. I don't know why I ran from him. He wasn't scary or mean or anything. Well, it doesn't matter. More tomorrow. Jill"

CHAPTER 5

Early the next morning, as the sun was rising over the town, I saw Jill walking toward the beach. The weather had gotten much warmer during the night. You could feel it; today was going to be a hot one.

Jill looked totally different. She had on light blue shorts and a boys white T shirt. She was much thinner than when we had seen her in the alley in long pants and a jacket. Her arms and legs were thin and pasty white. Her bare feet were thin and bony. As she crossed Bay Avenue, a book fell from her hand. When she bent down to pick it up, she grabbed a piece of broken oyster shell. She faced the bay and skimmed the shell across the flat surface of the calm water.

On the beach, at the end of Randolph is a wooden six-sided shelter that some would call a gazebo. The town's folk know it as The Pavilion and it has become the symbol of the Town of Cape Charles. Jill climbed the sand hill at the edge of the street and walked to it. The concrete floor was miserably cold and wet with condensation. It felt slimy beneath her feet and she scurried through it to the other side. The soft sand was much warmer and the morning chill would soon be gone.

I left Jill at the beach and flew east to Fig Street to see if Skeeter was up and moving around. He was up all right. He had his baseball, glove, and bat balanced in the basket of his bike. He was already tired of the cast on his arm.

At least it covered only his forearm and not his elbow too. He could still put his glove on his hand and he managed to catch and he could hit a little too.

"Cack." I zoomed past his head and lit on the ground nearby. I was hoping he brought something from breakfast for me.

"Here, Rue" Skeeter held out his hand and showed me three small pieces of toast, damp with melted butter.

"Cack. Cack"

He tossed the toast in my direction and climbed on his bike. I kept an eye on him while I pecked at my breakfast.

"There has to be somebody to play ball with, Rue." Skeeter peddled through town hoping to find anyone to do something with.

"Be-bop-a-lula, she's my baby, be-bop-a-lula, I don't mean maybe."

Skeeter sang to himself. He had no clue anyone within a hundred yards could hear the self-proclaimed "teen idol." He told me several times that he had to see Gene Vincent in person to find out what he did that made girls go screaming wild. I wasn't sure why Skeeter would even want to know why Gene made girls go crazy. Such a mystery.

I feel terrible, telling you Bud, I mean betraying a friend's trust. But, after all, it is my story to tell. He'll get over it anyway.

I flew over the school and park. Both were empty. No kids anywhere. Skeeter sang and continued west on

Tazewell. We got to the beach and there was no one moving around except a few grown-ups walking a dog.

Maybe this is it. I remembered Jill at the pavilion earlier. Maybe I can get them to talk. Nah. No way, that's gonna happen.

Skeeter rode up the incline to the walkway that separated the beach from the street. The water was calm, barely moving at all. Sort of like the town. Skeeter cut loose a louder version of "BE-BOP-A-LULA." He closed one eye and saw himself on a huge stage.

He coasted into the shade of the pavilion and flipped the kick stand on his bike. He looked in all directions making sure no one was in sight. In the center of the shelter he posed with his eyes closed tight. He counted off to the Blue Caps. Uh, oh, Gene Attack!

"One, two, three, four, one, two, weeeeellllllllllll, be-bop-a-lula, she's my baby, be-bop-a-lula, I don't mean maybe." He wailed.

Skeet *was* Gene. There were hundreds, no, thousands of screaming teen aged girls in tight sweaters. Jumping up and down, many had tears in their eyes. Stern- faced police formed a human barrier in front of the stage. Skeeter winked at one of them as a gesture of good will and thanks for protecting him from the masses. 'Gene' strutted for his fans, strumming his guitar and gyrating like a kid juiced up on Kool Aid.

This was hysterical. Poor Skeeter. He was a terrible singer, he couldn't dance, and his summer buzz cut didn't make it as the hair of a teen idol. I felt it my duty to warn him of approaching passersby. There were none, so I let the boy have at it.

I was wrong. Boy, how I was wrong. Skeeter couldn't see over the sand dunes that separated the Pavilion from the shore. From my lookout, I couldn't see either.

And, it wasn't until I saw her hair, then her forehead, then her eyes, that I knew Jill had been sitting on the beach reading. Behind the dune, she had been out of sight. Now, she was walking around the sand to see the source of the moaning she was hearing.

When I saw her, I started flapping my wings like I'd been shot. I went air born and shot in front of the teen idol. Skeeter strummed his baseball bat like a guitar. He wouldn't quit. I buzzed him again. He sang with greater intensity. His face, red with rocker energy, glistened with sweat. It wasn't a pretty sight. Then 'Gene' finished his most famous song and bowed humbly to the applause and cheers of adoring fans.

Actually, there was only one person in the audience, since it looked as if I had been part of the show too. I was embarrassed for both of us.

Skeeter opened his eyes to blow kisses to his adoring fans. But wait. There was no band. There were no girls in form-fitting sweaters. And, it wasn't until he heard a girl's laughter, he realized it wasn't a boy pointing at him.

Not one of the three of us knew what to do next. Skeeter and I wished we were somewhere else.

Jill had never seen anything like this in Lee County. What this kid was screaming was nothing like the county and blue grass music she was used to. He sounded like a cross between a Holy Roller and a pig at slaughter. His spastic gyrations made her think she was finally seeing somebody pitching a conniption fit. It must be something about Skeeter's family, where throwing fits is not an unusual occurrence.

He spied the getaway car. It wasn't a limousine waiting for him and the Blue Caps, just his bike. He fumbled with it and it fell on its side. The baseball equipment spilled out onto the floor. He struggled with his one and a half arms to set it upright, grab the bat, and stuff the glove in the basket. He watched the ball roll, as if it had a mind of its own, straight in Jill's direction.

Jill was laughing like a hyena now. I was perched in the rafters of The Pavilion waiting for Skeeter to make a break for it.

"What you lookin' at, black bird?" Jill looked up at me.

I thought it best to drop down from the rafters and glide out of the shelter. I flapped and flew as fast as I could to catch up with Skeeter. I turned my head to see Jill standing in the sand holding the baseball high in the air.

"You forgot your ball!" She yelled.

CHAPTER 6

Skeeter scorned his reflection in the mirror over his dresser. "Idiot. You idiot."

He smacked his forehead with the heel of his hand. Letting himself fall backward on his bed, "Y O U I D I O T" he spelled the two words out loud. "Why did I do that?"

It wasn't so much a question as it was a statement of disgust with himself.

I tried to stop you. I wished I could say. All I could do was stand on his window sill and watch him deal with his embarrassment.

"Rueben, if that girl tells Shad or Peanut, or anybody about this, I'll never live it down. I'm doomed."

Skeeter opened his dresser drawer and got out his Gene Vincent record and the magazines with stories about him and the Blue Caps. He read the articles for the millionth time. He put "BE-BOP-A-LULA" on and listened.

I'll just tell her I'm a student of modern music and I was practicing to be in a play. Yea, that's what I'll do. Skeeter smiled. Then he frowned. He looked me in the eye and said. "It don't matter. I'll probably never talk to her anyway. I hope I never see her again. Then, the whole thing will be over."

While Skeeter was feeling sorry for himself, I took flight. I was hungry for something other than the cracked corn that Mr. Floyd, the man who cared for me as a baby crow, always kept out for me. There are a couple of pecan trees on Pine Street. I can usually find a few pecans scattered around the ground. I flew over the park on the way to the pecan feast. It seemed odd that the kids Skeeter played with every summer were not around.

Who's that on the ball field? I wondered. Somebody was standing on the pitcher's mound tossing a ball up in the air then catching it. I flew in a huge circle around the field. I stopped every so often to get a better look. The ball was thrown high in the air again and again. As I got closer, I recognized the pitcher. I knew exactly who it was.

"You spyin'on me, black bird?" She yelled in my direction.

I sailed straight ahead for the cover of several oaks. I wasn't sure she wouldn't try to peg me with the ball, right in mid air. Jill shouted at me. "Where's your hot shot friend?" The girl, I mean Jill, put the ball in her glove and rested both hands on her skinny hips. She stood facing me like she was trying to stare me down. "Hey bird, you scared of me too?"

Uh oh, I thought, she's a feisty one.

I knew Skeeter was lonesome. Maybe I could get them together, even though they were off to a rocky start. I didn't have anything to lose.

I flapped my wings and jumped off my branch and glided as slowly as I could in a circle around her. Then, a small dust cloud rose around my feet as I hit the infield. I was about fifteen feet from her.

"Cack"

"Cack, to you." She mocked me. Jill squatted on her heels. She looked me over good. I felt a little uncomfortable but she made me feel OK. I suppose she thought I meant her no harm. Her sweet smile and the twinkle in her eyes made me wonder just how tough she really was.

I walked back and forth in front of her trying not to do something stupid. Maybe I could get her to walk over to Skeeter's house. I flapped hard again.

Whoosh, whoosh.

I flew in a small circle toward Skeeter's house.

"Cack. Cack."

"Where you goin', bird?"

"Cack." I said.

I flew higher then sank lower again, never getting behind her. I wanted her to chase me in Skeeter's direction. I flew high then crossed in front of her then toward Skeeter's, just a few yards at a time.

She must have caught on to the game. Now she was trotting along nicely as I flew ahead and teased her into following me. When we got to Nectarine Street she began to loose interest. She stopped and remembered the baseball.

Uh-oh. I thought. It's over.

She tossed the ball a few times and caught it. Then she took a mighty wind up and threw it with all her might. It actually hummed as it cut through the air on its way back to the ball field.

"Bye, bird." Jill put her hind legs in overdrive and high tailed it back to the pitcher's mound.

Well, maybe it's just not meant to be. I should probably mind my own business. I can't do that. I'm too curious.

Jill retrieved the ball she threw from the outfield. She walked to the pitcher's mound and began a wind up. Before she hurled it, she stopped in mid stride. She studied the spot where she saw kids huddled around a hurt kid on her first day in town. I wonder if the teen idol with the broken arm is the same kid I saw at the school? It must be the same kid. He must live near here.

Jill walked back to Nectarine where she had left me. It was one block from there to the end of town. She tossed the ball in the air as she walked and looked for Skeeter's bike.

Skeeter had slipped past me while I was trying to lure Jill to his house. He probably went back to the Pavilion to see if Jill had left his ball somewhere nearby. All he found was a candy wrapper and a book. The title of the book was, *Favorite Seaside Cooking.*

He looked inside for the owner's name. There was none. Maybe Mom can use this, he thought.

Skeeter peddled north to Tazewell. Passing Peach, he thought he saw someone at the ball field throwing a ball. Excited about the possibility of playing ball with somebody, he turned his bike around and headed toward the field. As he got to the clearing at the end of Peach, he saw someone tossing a ball all right.

"Oh, no." Skeeter shouted at me. "It's her."

Jill spotted Skeeter about the same time he saw her. "Hey kid. Here's your ball." Jill yelled at him.

Skeeter cringed. Oh, jeez, what do I do now? What a loud mouth. She has no manners. None. I knew what he was thinking. He got off his bike and pushed it through the clover that grew around the infield.

Jill held the scuffed baseball. "You forgot to get your ball this morning."

Skeeter cut his eyes to look at her but didn't move his head. Jill held the ball straight out in front of him. She had a smirky grin. It was a grin that told him she knew he had made a fool of himself.

Skeeter looked down and mumbled. "Thanks."

He reached out and grabbed the ball being careful not to touch her fingers. He waited for her to let it go but she didn't.

"Thanks." He said louder.

He had to look up at her, I thought. "Be a man, Skeeter! Be a man!" I wished he knew what I was thinking.

"You gonna let go?" He looked at her.

"Don't know yet. How about we arm wrestle for it?"

"What?"

"Can't you arm wrestle?"

"Well, sure. I just don't want to hurt' cha."

"Ah, ha, ha. Hurt me? Hurt me?"

While the humiliation continued in Skeeter's mind, Jill stuck her right leg behind Skeeter's knees and shoved the ball and his arm straight back at him. Skeeter hit the ground hard. He was overwhelmed, well confused. It was the worst disgrace possible in a boy's world. Taken down by a girl. A girl!

"You ain't gonna hurt me. So don't you ever think about it again."

Skeeter nearly blurted out something totally stupid like, "yes, sir."

Jill dropped the ball and grabbed Skeeter's still empty, still outstretched hand. "Let me help you up, Sport."

I could tell Skeeter wanted to throw her down good and hard. He knew he shouldn't try. What if he really caused her to break her head or something? "I can get up by myself."

"Well, I know you can Ace. I was just tryin' to be nice."

Skeeter helped himself up and brushed dirt off his butt. "Where'd you come from, anyway?"

Jill stood with her hands on her hips. She twisted her head to the right and spit through the gap in her two front teeth. "Lee County Virginia," she said.

Skeeter kicked a dirt clod then looked back at her. "What cha' doin' here?"

"My daddy heard there was work here and we got kin up in Maryland."

"Where'd you git that glove?"

"It was my brother's. He gave it to me." Jill squeezed the baseball tight in her throwing hand. "Can you catch with that broken arm?"

Skeeter was starting to hate the cast. "As long as it ain't a line drive."

"Wanna throw some then?" She twitched her nose at him.

Over the next two hours they played catch, took batting practice, and hit grounders and fly balls. It made me happy that they got along. Skeeter told her about Wenus, Shadrack, Peanut, and what school was like.

Jill told him about where she had lived. When she told him about how her mother had died, Skeeter got a big knot in his throat. Jill's eyes got red when she told him about how much she missed her. Even though she didn't cry, it was all Skeeter could do not to. He couldn't imagine not having one of his parents anymore.

He changed the subject. "Wanna go to my house and get somethin' to drink?" They needed a break from such a sad story.

Jill hadn't been inside any house in Cape Charles but hers and the lady's who gave her the parsley,

Skeeter tilted his bike upright and put their baseball stuff in the basket.

"Hey, that's my book." Jill reached for it.

Skeeter pushed the bike away from her. He tried to hop on and start peddling to tease her. "Your name's not in it. It's mine."

"Bull!"

Skeeter was pumping the bike peddles like mad, but he didn't get enough of a head start. Jill caught up with him and snatched it from the basket. Skeeter tried to turn the handlebars away, but she was too quick. He lost his balance and he and the bike were thrown flat to the ground.

"Hey, Clyde. I told you it was mine."

Skeeter was laughing and Jill grinned like a mad man. I buzzed Skeeter then landed on the ground nearby, turned away from them, and smiled too. Since we don't have lips to smile with, crows open their beaks and wiggle their tongues when something pleases them.

"Cack. Cack."

"What's with the black bird?" Jill stared at me.

"That's Rueben. He's an American crow."

Skeeter told Jill the basic story of how I got into town. He told her that we were friends and we had a lot of fun together.

"Hi Rueben. My name's Jill."

"I like your name." Skeeter said. "My cousin had a dog named Jill. I liked it as a dog's name too."

"Gee, thanks. I'm glad I remind you of a dog.

"Wait. You don't remind me of a dog. Your name does. I mean all I mean is...."

"It's OK, Clyde. I know what you mean."

"Stop callin' me Clyde." He said.

Jill stood in front of Skeeter with her hand on her hips. "Well, what's your name then?"

"Skeeter."

"Mosquiter?" Jill snickered.

Skeeter's lip curled up as he stared back at her. "Hardy, har. It's Skeeter."

"I saw you right after you got your arm broke."

"How do you mean?" He said.

Jill pointed to the infield. "It was over there. They were helpin' you up. It was the day we moved here."

They crossed Plum Street and shuffled along the grassy median of Monroe Avenue. Skeeter's house was the second one from Fig Street. It was brick, it had a basement, and it was two stories tall. There was a slate roof and four dormers with colored glass windows.

Skeeter led the way to the back yard. I flew around the side of the house too and stopped near an old metal bowl that Skeeter kept filled with water. "Come on."

Skeeter climbed the brick steps to the kitchen, flung the screen door open and walked in. Jill didn't follow him. The screen door slammed shut. He looked at her through the screen. "What's wrong?"

"Am I supposed to come too?"

"Sure."

She took a deep breath. "I've never been in a house this nice before."

She kept her hands at her sides. Her brown eyes took in the yellow walls and the bright white wood trim. She studied the dishes that she could see, all matched and were neatly stacked in the correct places. "Your mom's got a lot of pots and pans."

"I guess. Open up the cupboards and look."

"I'd better not."

Skeeter held out a glass. "You want water or milk?"

"I don't care."

He poured two medium size glasses of milk. They each took a couple of gulps.

"Hey, try this. I invented a snack." Skeeter said, and opened the pantry door. He took out a package of dinner rolls. From another cupboard, he produced a bottle of corn syrup and unscrewed the cap. "Now do this."

Jill watched as Skeeter held the roll with one side pointing up. He stuck his finger into the soft roll until it got to the center. Her eyes widened when she saw him pour the clear syrup into the hole. He filled it to the top and held it until the thick sticky syrup was soaked into the bread. When it was all soaked in, he started eating it. His new friend laughed at him eating it, but did exactly as he had.

"S'good ain't it?" Skeeter's cheeks stretched around the dinner roll in his mouth.

Jill stuffed the rest of her roll in her mouth and chewed like mad. She shook her head from side to side. "No," she muttered through the gooey treat

After swallowing a few times, they wiped their milk mustaches on their sleeves. Skeeter rinsed the glasses out and set them in the sink.

"Will you tell me somethin'?" Jill looked at her new friend.

"I guess." He said.

"What were you doin' this morning'?" She was trying her best not to laugh.

"Jeez. Sorry."

"That was the funniest thing I ever saw. Show me again what you were doin'."

She couldn't help it now. She was laughing right in front of him. I watched them through the screen. I still cocked my head away when I felt a crow smile coming on.

Skeeter was a little embarrassed, but, he let her laugh. Once she calmed down, he walked to the short flight of stairs leading to a landing.

"OK. I'll show you. Come on."

Up the second flight of stairs, then left at the hall, the first door on the right was Skeeter's room. A much larger room than Jill's, Skeeter had a double bed, not a single cot like hers. Skeeter had been taught to make his bed every morning and to keep his things in order. A plastic ship model and an airplane model were on his dresser. Next to them was a piggy bank that was actually shaped and painted like a pig. 'For My Boat' was painted on the side with lady's red nail polish.

"Listen to this." Skeeter stood next to his record player. He switched it on and they watched the arm automatically lift itself up, turn to the left, and position the needle precisely at the beginning of the record.

"Weeellllll......, be-bop-a-lula, she's my baby, be-bop-a-lula, I don't mean maybe." Gene and the Blue Caps belted it once again.

I flew up to Skeeter's window and stood on the sill. Skeeter grinned and sang along with Gene. Not too loudly, though. Jill tapped her feet and thumbed through the Gene magazine articles. They listened to it five times straight.

"I love that." Jill finally spoke.

They spent the next half hour listening to the record. Skeeter told her everything that he knew about Gene and rock' n 'roll.

"Now look at this." Skeeter pulled open the top drawer of his desk and took out a newspaper. "Gene Vincent Coming to Norfolk Arena," was the heading of another Gene article.

"I'm goin' to see him."

Jill seemed as excited as Skeeter. "You are?"

"Yea, I'm saving any money I can get. I have to buy my own ticket and pay for any stuff I want to eat there. My dad said he'd drive me but I have to pay the ferry fare both ways."

"Lucky. I never saw anybody famous. Well, my Uncle Cooter did win a hog callin' contest at the county fair last year. And, I seen him a billion times."

"Great," Skeeter mumbled.

CHAPTER 7

That night during dinner, I walked around the porch outside the dining room as usual, waiting for Skeeter to toss me something from their meal.

"Well, it's time to look for the house keys," Skeeter's dad announced. "I remember putting them away somewhere. I put them where I could find them easily this year."

Like most people in town, they rarely locked their doors.

"Are we going on a vacation?" Skeeter asked.

"No, this is different. Mr. Bundick told me today that a friend of his down in Norfolk saw a band of gypsies working their way north from Florida, coming toward Cape Charles."

"Wha…? What about gypsies, Dad?"

"Aw, they're a bunch of ne'er-do-wells who travel south for the winter and back north again in the summer. They have dark skin and they all have long black hair. Even the men; they have pierced ears. Imagine that? Even the tiniest of babies have pierced ears. And the women have long black hair growing from their arm pits."

"That's enough." Skeeter's mom said sternly. We rarely heard Skeeter's mother be so bold with his father. "That's not a very pleasant topic for the dinner table." She added.

For some reason the gypsies kept popping in and out of Skeeter's thoughts that night. The next morning Skeeter came outside and straddled his bike. "Let's go exploring, Rue." Skeeter called out.

Skeeter aimed his bike along Fig Street, then east on Stone Road, out of town. The railroad shops were just out of town, next to the train tracks and parallel to the road.

Everyone passed this building going in and out of town.

"Bang, bang, bang," over and over we heard the pounding of heavy steel hammers slamming into the steel wheel assemblies of a huge train engine. All of the train maintenance was done by mechanics and craftsmen who worked from one of the shops. I was born in this building and although the noise was frightening, I always felt comfortable passing by. About half way from the train shops and the highway we saw a bluish gray haze drifting from a pine thicket. Skeeter's nose picked up the scent of wood smoke.

"Probably a hobo cooking his lunch," Skeeter said out loud.

Lots of men hopped trains all over the country and many passed through Cape Charles. Although Skeeter was taught to be friendly, he was cautioned many times not to befriend any drifters on his own. Keeping away from a hobo camp was easy for him to do. He was warned and now wanted to have nothing to do with them. Further down the road, Skeeter stopped his bike when he thought he heard guitar music. There were other interesting sounds too. I hopped onto the handlebars and listened.

"It sounds like metal things clanging together or bells or something." Skeeter said to me. "It sounds like music, but nothing like I've never heard. What is it?"

Skeeter decided to follow the sounds, get a little closer, and investigate. Even if it were just hobos, he knew that he would be able to get away without being seen. Not-being seen by hobos was one thing, but not being seen by anyone else was a different story. Almost everyone in Cape Charles knew Skeeter and if even one person saw him, it would be all over town that he was sneaking around in the woods. His parents would be furious; he'd be put on restriction, and probably get a belt whack from his father too. But, he could always tell his parents that they had instilled a love of music in him and he couldn't resist finding out what kind of music it was. Yea, that's pretty good. Skeeter thought to himself and smiled at his brilliance. Now back to business.

He pushed his bike into some wild blackberry bushes. He bent the rear view mirror face down. Now, it couldn't reflect the sun's rays and attract anyone's attention.

"Ouch. Jeez. Dang it," he said. Skeeter felt the sting of the bushes' needle tipped thorns. The harder he tried to get free, the more tangled he became. It was as if the thorns had lives of their own and their goal was to punish him for invading wild blackberry territory. The battle with the thorns ended in a tie. Skeeter finally freed himself, but suffered ripped skin, torn pants, and a shredded shirt. The blackberry bush resumed its life with a few broken branches and several bloody threads of glory.

Chapter 7

Skeeter's arms and hands stung as his salty sweat mixed into his wounds. He yanked his blue and white handkerchief from his back pocket and mashed it against his cuts.

What a mess. He was covered by road dust and now had blood smeared all over. He had come this far now and he was determined to find the music and the musicians.

Pretending he was spying on train robbers, he took his sod buster out of his pocket, but didn't open the blade. Since he'd had trouble with the thorns, he figured he'd better not be too stupid and run with a knife in his hand. He would surely trip and fall on it, impaling himself and he'd croak alone, and without any significant reason other than being nosey.

I kept hidden and watched him bend over as low as he could. He scooted behind clumps of bushes, tall grass, and saplings. The music got louder then softer as the bay wind changed direction. Soon he was close enough to find a more permanent place to spy. He peeked over a long abandoned piece of rusted farm machinery and kept quiet as possible. Now, he understood why the music he was hearing was so different from anything he had heard before. The entire scene was most unusual.

There in the sunshine was a lady wearing a long, flowing skirt and a pure white blouse. Dancing in perfect rhythm with the strum of a guitar, we could only see her when she passed between the four old cars parked in a circle.

The lady had long black hair that hung down her back to her belt. She wore bright red lipstick and red rouge on her cheeks. And the oddest thing, she had little brass cymbals on her thumbs and middle fingers. She tapped her fingers and thumbs together at the appropriate times, just as the guitar and words required. Both the lady and a man sang along in a foreign language. He had never seen or heard such a thing. Oh, no, he thought, gypsies. He had no idea how many others were there. What if they're watching us? What if they capture me? He thought. What if they take me with them? What if they force me to become a gypsy too? What if they sell me? I gotta' git outta' here.

All of this thinking took about two seconds. Still clutching his sod buster he made himself flat on the ground, face down. Planning to make a run for it, we heard a bass drum beat. But, it didn't keep the same beat as the music. The bass drum he heard was actually his heart pounding against the hard dry earth.

"Somethin' stinks." Skeeter whispered and scrunched his nose up between his eyes. "Oh, no. It's cow manure."

Then, I smelled it too. Skeeter had crawled across a fresh cow pie. If I hadn't been so worried about him, I'd have laughed like crazy. He couldn't do anything about it now. He'd surely be discovered. He raised himself up into a squatting stance and quietly moved toward his bike's hiding place. I watched him move to the base of a tall pine tree and slither around it so he could stand up, hidden by its trunk.

Chapter 7

He slid up the trunk of the rough bark and pressed his back against it. We were not alone.

"What did you think you were looking at? Why are you sneakin' around and spying on people? You think you're at a circus or some kind of freak show? Huh? Huh?"

Skeeter nearly wet his pants. He saw in front of him a tall huge man dressed in black with black hair and the whitest teeth he'd ever seen. When he heard the first words, Skeeter slammed his eyes shut and squeezed the lids until they hurt. He was certain he would soon feel a board slam into his head and be knocked out, all because of being nosey.

Wait a minute, Skeeter thought, his eyes now burning. That's no man. His eyes sprang open. He wasn't knocked out. Still standing in front of him, with the meanest look that he could portray, was a boy balancing on an old clam basket. A gypsy kid, Skeeter thought.

"Well?" the boy barked. "What do you want here?" the boy demanded.

"I heard music that I'd never heard before."

"Liar," the boy barked again. "Are you a sheriff or somebody like that?" he asked Skeeter.

"What?" Asked Skeeter.

The boy stared angrily at Skeeter. "I'll bet you're the law, come looking for us."

"I ain't no law," Skeeter said. "I'm a boy like you're a boy." Skeeter then noticed that the boy dressed in black was shaking as much as he was. Skeeter didn't let on that he knew the boy was as scared of Skeeter as much as Skeeter was of the boy.

"Did your arms get bloody from arresting somebody?" Gypsy boy asked.

"No," Skeeter said, "I don't even know how to arrest somebody. Look, I just wanted to see who was making that music. I got caught in thorns when I was hidin' my bike."

"Why did you think you had to hide?" the boy asked.

"Well....two reasons. I didn't want to be no where near a hobo camp and I didn't want anyone to know that I was being nosey."

"So, then. Did you see enough?" The boy was still angry.

"I guess so." Skeeter answered.

Neither of them knew what to say or do next. There was a staring match. Well, it started as a staring match but the longer they stared it was becoming less and less of one to either boy. They stared at each other for a long time, sizing each other up. "Everybody calls me Skeeter. I gotta go."

"Go then. And, you stink." The gypsy ordered.

Skeeter backed up a little, looked at the poop on his pants and started walking away. But, he kept the boy in sight as he moved toward the road and his bike. When Skeeter was almost out of hearing range, he heard the boy yell out.

"Hey, Skeeter. Come back tomorrow."

"I don't think so." Skeeter yelled back. Come back tomorrow? What was that about?

CHAPTER 8

During the next week or so Skeeter, Jill, and I roamed around town. I was happy to have something new to do, and I was delighted that Skeeter would no longer be miserable trying to entertain himself. Skeeter and Jill played ball, raced each other, arm wrestled, swam in the bay and searched for sea glass along its shore. The best thing that happened was they developed a friendship, trusting and true.

Jill told Skeeter and me about her mother and how she taught Jill about herbs and cooking when Jill was very young. "Momma used to show me all kinds of things about cookin' and spices. She told me how important it was to keep your husband happy by cooking good food for him every night. A husband, for Pete's sake, imagine that. When Momma died, I didn't care much about anything for a long time. I love my daddy and brothers and everything like that. But with Momma gone, I'm more or less like the three of them. We all pitch in to make ends meet." Jill looked through Skeeter like he wasn't even there.

Skeeter interrupted the silence. "I can't imagine having only one of my parents. I'm sorry about your momma."

"My daddy and brothers do real good takin' care of me. I miss Momma real bad, though."

Jill then focused her eyes on Skeeter. "Don't you never tell nobody this. I never let Daddy or my brothers know when I get sad about Momma. I never let them see me cry when I miss her so bad either. I never cry in front of them. And I never act like a girl."

"Why don't you want to act like a girl?"

Jill looked down at her feet.

"I don't ever want anybody feelin' sorry for me. I just want to be like a regular person. And, just because I told you this secret stuff, you gotta' promise not to treat me different cause I ain't got no momma. Do you promise?"

"OK." Skeeter promised. "Shake on it."

Jill returned the hand shake but kept squeezing Skeeter's hand until he pushed her away. She wouldn't let go. Staring each other down, they positioned their feet into an Indian wrestling position. They pushed and pulled each other's arms until their laughter overtook their wrestling skills. They each gave up at the same time and collapsed on the ground in hysterics.

As the summer passed, Jill met some of the other kids who lived in Cape Charles. Throughout the summer, most of the kids headed off to summer camps, to visit relatives, or to go on family vacations. Skeeter told her about life on the shore. She learned that since the ferries were moved south to Kiptopeke and the railroad lost its passenger service, Cape Charles had begun to die. People moved away to find work in other places. Now, just as in the beginning, even before the town was built, the people who lived here earned a hard living. Being a farmer or a waterman was what the shore was about.

"Your dad's lucky he got a job here." Skeeter told her.

"I feel lucky to live here. I like it so far." Jill said.

Soon after Skeeter believed he could trust Jill as a friend, he led her outside the town limits. Jill walked next to him. "Where're we goin'?"

"You made me promise not to tell anybody about you, so I'm gonna' show you somethin' that's special to me." He said.

I flew in circles high over head and searched the fields and Kings Creek ahead of us. Of course, I knew Skeeter was going to take Jill to his boat. The tiny row boat had been his dad's. When Skeeter had proven his ability to row and maneuver it safely, it had become his. It was Skeeter's most precious procession. Since Jill had confided in him, Skeeter wanted to share his love of his boat with her.

They left Washington Avenue at the east end of town and made their way through the field to King's Creek. At a small wooden pier, weathered gray by the wind and the water, Jill was introduced to Skeeter's boat. "What's her name?" She asked him.

"Who?"

"The boat, what's the boat's name? She has to have a name."

"I never named her." He answered. He wondered why he'd never thought about it.

Skeeter's boat sat proud in the water. The hull was white and the pale blue trim made her look perfect. Skeeter kept the boat ship shape and touched up the paint whenever it got damaged. It was quite a contrast to the well worn look of the fishing boats tied up at the town's harbor.

"Can I name her?" Jill got excited about the possibilities.

"I guess." Skeeter wondered how this was going to end.

"I know, Annie Oakley," she said. "No, Calamity Jane. No, wait."

"No. You wait." Skeeter said. "You can't name her without riding in her first."

"Says who?"

"Says me. She's my boat!"

"I got it. How about 'Spirit'?" Jill's eyes sparkled as she looked skyward.

"That's dumb." Skeeter was quick to answer. "How did you think that up?"

"It ain't dumb. My mom. My mom used to call me 'Spirit' a lot. She would call me 'Happy Spirit.' Once when I was sad about somethin' she called me 'Blue Spirit'."

"Yea? Well, I don't know. I'll have to think about it." Skeeter was in no mood to think of boat names anyway. Maybe I'll name her, 'Be Bop', he thought.

"When you get that cast off, will you show me how to dig clams? I want to try out a recipe for clam fritters that's in my book?"

"Sure. But let's go for a ride now."

CHAPTER 9

When he woke the next morning, it seemed like only a few minutes had gone by since he'd flopped into bed. Skeeter pulled his swimming suit on and hopped down the stairs to the kitchen.

"Don't forget to eat your breakfast" his mother said.

"OK, Mom." Skeeter dropped two pieces of bread into the slots on top of the chrome toaster. When the bread turned to toast, he smeared some apple butter on one side real thick and squeezed down the other piece on top so they stuck together. He swallowed a glass of milk. Then he wrapped the toast he'd just made and the toast from his mother's plate in waxed paper and went out the back door to get his bike. He grabbed his wire basket and clam rakes and loaded everything into an old wooden crate that he had mounted above his rear fender.

Skeeter told his mom goodbye and headed toward Kings Creek. He knew a great place to clam. It was up the bay about a mile north of town. At Kings Creek he got off his bike and leaned it against a tall pine tree. The plan was for Jill to meet him there where Skeeter kept the boat with no name. She had begged him to teach her how to find clams. Skeeter, for some reason, had just never planned to take anyone with him, especially a girl. Actually, until they had become friends, he had never though about girls other than how annoying they could be. Jill hadn't annoyed him yet. Also, he hadn't thought much abut Jill being a girl anyway. It was only since his obsession with Gene Vincent that Skeeter had become fascinated with the thought of girls. Real rock 'n' roll girls, who one day would be screaming for him and his smooth singing, like they did for Gene.

Unless Jill remembered to bring the lunch as she said she would, he was determined to cut this clamming lesson short and be back as soon as possible. All he brought was the toast, a canteen of water, and the tools they needed for clam digging.

After putting the supplies in his boat, Skeeter stepped from the weathered gray pier into the center of the boat. His weight made the boat sit lower in the water with him and the stuff in it. He watched as water oozed into the boat between the boards of the boat's sides. He knew that after a while each board would swell up with water and press themselves to each adjoining one. When that happened, the water couldn't get inside of the boat as fast as it was coming in now. Once Jill got in, the whole process started again until the next higher boards swelled to their original shape. Skeeter kept a tin can in the boat to bail out the water when it got too deep. He poured water onto the sides so that the boards would start their swelling before Jill got there.

Skeeter and his father had spent many hours together on the creeks and along the bay side of the shore. Since he was five years old, he spent most of his summer days watching people and learning about coastal life. He knew how to fish with a pole, line, hook, and float. He also knew how to catch fish using a seine net. He had been on oyster boats and watched the men drop their huge tongs straight down beside their boats. He had made his own crab pot from scrap metal and wire that he found and worked like a champ.

Skeeter knew how to clean and cook what he caught too. He was taught early not to waste what he'd caught. If his family couldn't eat all he caught, he would give the rest to anyone who needed something to eat.

That's just how it is. Skeeter thought. The life he knew was about people on the shore sharing everything with each other, especially gossip.

Skeeter didn't hear Jill when she snuck through the field to where he docked his boat. She found a tall reed from a cattail and brought it with her. While Skeeter was wetting down the boat she moved in silence, inching herself toward him. She crouched down and made herself as small as possible. Secretly she slid the reed from her hiding place over the boat's stern. The tip of the reed bobbed up way too high and she had to bring it closer to her and start over. Again, she pushed the reed at the back of the boy's head. Skeeter's hand rocketed up and smacked his ear. It happened so fast Jill barely got the reed out of the path of flight without him hitting it. She let a few seconds go by then stretched her arm out again and touched him with it in almost the same spot. Up came Skeeter's hand and, "smack" he slapped his ear again. Jill jerked the reed real fast again. She was nearly in tears with laughter and fought hard to keep it inside. On the third attempt she couldn't control herself. At the tickle of his ear, Skeeter slapped it again. This time he trapped the reed to his head and spun around at lightning speed. Jill burst out in hysterical laughter, tears now running down her cheeks. She fell over backward on the sand and howled.

"You, jackass!" Skeeter shouted as he rubbed his throbbing ear.

We watched her roll in the sand in hysterics. And when he pictured what he must have looked like slapping his head, he started to laugh too.

Jill sat up. "Whew Skeet head, that was a good one."

"Don't call me Skeet head." He said. "You, you, you.......Jilly jelly head."

Jill fell back to the sand again and cried with laughter. Falling backward she pointed to Skeeter's ear. "You're ear is cherry red. Ah, ha, ha. Ah, ha, ha. I mean *CHERRY RED!* Ah, ha, ha, ha, ha. Ah, ha, ha. Whew."

Skeeter walked up to his bicycle and looked at his ear in the rear view mirror. He started to laugh all over again. It took Jill a long time to settle down to where they could talk normal again.

Since Jill didn't have a bike, she had lugged the box and contents all the way from her house on Peach Street.

"*Peach* Street," Skeeter mumbled to himself. Jill hated the fact that she lived on *Peach* Street.

She once told him, "It sounds like a girly-girl street." Jill by no means wanted to have anything to do with being a girly girl. It didn't seem like a big deal to Skeeter, but it gave him something to tease her about.

She had set the box on the sand next to his bike. Skeeter picked it up and walked back toward the scene of her practical joke. Jill was standing now, looking at the boat. She had regained control of herself. She wore short pants and a ragged boy's shirt. Sand stuck to the back of her head, her legs, and to her clothes.

"I brought your things down." Skeeter said. "You ready to cross the creek?"

"Yea."

Skeeter saw the sand all over her. "Why don't you brush the sand off yourself?"

"If it bothers you so much, why don't you brush it off? You're not the boss of me."

You're not the boss of me, Skeeter mocked her to himself. He wondered why he even agreed to take her clamming in the first place.

Skeeter slipped the worn rope from the cleat that was screwed to the dock. He pushed his hands against the dock and they started moving. The boat said goodbye to the pier as if it were happy to be going on an adventure. Skeeter sat on the middle seat and rowed while Jill perched on the bow. It took only a few minutes to row the tiny boat across the creek.

Skeeter stared into the water. "Do you think I'm really gonna' see Gene?"

"Sure. If you work hard enough for somethin', you can make it come true. Or, at least, help yourself along the way. See? I kept beggin' you to teach me how to find clams and here we are."

I flew ahead, excited about the possibilities for lunch. When they arrived, he ordered Jill to hop out and pull the rope toward shore. The water was perfect. They pulled the line together and moved the boat as far onto the sand as they safely could. If they went too far on the beach, the tide would go out farther and they wouldn't be able to get the boat back into the water.

Skeeter had been clamming with his parents a thousand times and had been a good student, and now he could be the teacher. He brought along enough burlap bags, the rough material that potato sacks were made of, to cover both the lunch box and the clam basket, provided they were lucky to catch any clams at all. He slid Jill's lunch box beneath the shade of some small trees up on the beach. He used one of the bags to cover it to protect it from the sun.

"Get the rakes." Skeeter said. "We'll put them in the basket and we'll each grab a handle."

With the wire clam basket suspended between them they waded along the shore of the great Chesapeake Bay.

Skeeter stopped and said, "Let's try here."

They set the basket down and each took a hand rake. Skeeter studied the wet sand as the water flowed onto the beach and then back out again. When tiny air bubbles floated up from the sand he took his rake and sunk the tines into the sand and pulled the rake toward him. Over and over he raked the wet sand and over and over and over again only sand, broken shells, and tiny sea creatures rushed between the tines. He sent Jill fifteen or twenty feet north of where he was.

"Be bop a lula, she's my baby. Be bop a lula, I don't mean maybe. Be bop a lula, she's my baby, be bop a lula, I don't mean maybe. Be bop a lula, she, e, e's my baby now, my baby now, my baby now." Skeeter sang the chorus.

Jill was too far away to hear him.

"I got two! I got two!" Jill called to him. Before he could hardly turn his head in her direction, she was running toward him with the clams. They were slightly bigger than silver dollars, the perfect size for bay side clams.

Dang it. Skeeter thought to himself. I should have known she'd get the first one. Just my luck. I can't beat her at anything.

I flew closer to inspect the catch.

"Cack." I approved.

Jill smiled at me and said, "Thanks, Rue. See?" Jill then showed them to Skeeter.

"Yea. They're great. They're perfect cherrystone clams." Skeeter said sarcastically. "Put them in the basket and sink it in the water. Then get the burlap wet and put it on top of them." Skeeter sounded like a teacher.

Jill set to work keeping the clams wet then went back to raking. After an hour, Jill had raked up two dozen. Skeeter had found thirteen. I could tell it irritated him because he was supposed to be the teacher.

Well, if I'm the teacher, the student did pretty well. He thought.

Jill's smile was so big that it made him stop thinking about how he should have been the one with the most clams. He was glad that it made her happy. Another thing was that she didn't even tease him about catching more…yet.

"Let's go. I'm gettin' hungry for that chicken salad." Skeeter said.

"Me, too."

They shared the weight of the basket and headed back to the boat. Jill waved her rake and splashed it along the surface of the water. Occasionally, when Skeeter wasn't looking she would aim the tines in Skeeter's direction and splash water on him. He didn't pay any attention to it until he could feel his shirt getting wetter.

She wondered how long she could splash water on him without him knowing it. He was busy thinking about the gypsy boy and the family camp. Then she made a mistake. She struck the water too hard with the rake. A huge spray hit him on the back of his head and on his back.

"You knot head." He yelled, "I'm drenched."

"Not yet, you're not." She said.

Before her words left her mouth, she let the basket of clams fall, dropped her rake, and lunged toward Skeeter. Skeeter's eyes opened wide as he realized she was going to take him down. He let go of the basket and tried to adjust his stance. Not in time though. Jill jumped behind him and had her hands on his shoulders before he could prepare for the inevitable. She pulled his shoulders down and pushed the back of his knees with her foot. Skeeter knew that he was done as soon as he heard her "not yet".

He held his cast high out of the water, but the rest of him was totally under water. He waved his cast like a madman struggling to keep it dry.

Jill yelled with laughter as she tried to get away from him. One step, then two. But on the third step Skeeter's hand clamped around her left ankle. He pulled hard halfway through her step.

"Noooo!" She screamed.

Still laughing from having dunked Skeeter, she hit the sandy bottom hard, face first. She sucked in a mouthful of water and tried to keep from swallowing it. She couldn't help it. She sucked bay water into her nose and felt it drip down the back of her throat. Gasping for breath, she lifted her head out of the water. Water shot out of her mouth and nose like a gargoyle fountain Skeeter once saw. Skeeter hooted and howled.

"How'd you like that, Knot Head?"

I became very concerned as Jill coughed and spit and gasped. She stood up and bent over putting her hands on her knees. Water kept running out of her nose. She blew it out of her nose without a handkerchief or anything. It was hysterical to Skeeter. Her face burned and her chin throbbed. Skeeter thought for a second that she may be really hurt Nah, he reminded himself. She started it and she was as tough as any boy in town.

Jill's chin stung and burned worse. Skeeter sat in the water about ten feet away in case she planned retaliation. He waited, what seemed like half an hour, for her to say something. Still bent over and staring down at the water, she saw a drop of blood fall from her face, dissolve and disappear onto the surface of the water. She wiped her chin with the palm of her wet hand. The blood diluted to a barely visible red. She brought a couple of handfuls of water to her face and washed the sand and grit away. Twice more she rinsed her face. Skeeter sat silently and watched blood drip from her chin. She took a couple of deep breaths and blew them out hard. She stood up straight, breathed hard again and caught her breath. She cocked her head to the side and spit.

She finally looked at Skeeter, got some half stupid grin on her face and said, "That was a good one."

He saw that grin and she looked like a Jill-o'-lantern.

A reflex laugh welled up inside her, but, instead of laughing, she snorted. After the snort, she coughed and snot flew out her nose and landed on Skeeter's leg. They each saw it at the same time. Jill pointed and howled once again. Skeeter looked down at it, turned toward the bay and ran as hard as he could, as if trying to get away from it. He ran until the water got too deep. He held his cast as high as he could and lowered the rest of himself into the water. He held his breath under the green water and rubbed his leg for all he was worth. When his leg was snot free he poked his head out of the water and took a huge breath. He spun toward the beach and saw Jill standing knee deep with her hands raised high above her head as if she had just won a foot race.

"Come on. Let's go, Snot Leg," she shouted.

"Aw, shut up Snot Nose," he yelled back. "You can see I'm comin'." Skeeter trudged through the surf until the water was only ankle deep.

"Whew, that was funny. That was so funny." Jill still chuckled.

They got the rakes, grabbed the handles of the clam basket, and headed with their catch back to the boat. They kicked the surf as they moved along the water's edge and occasionally laughed. Each knew what the other was thinking.

"My chin sure does burn." Jill said.

"Good. Let me see."

They stopped and Skeeter moved to stand in front of her. She held her head up and Skeeter stared at her red chin like a doctor would do. "Uh-oh."

"What?" Jill asked. "What?" She didn't care if it left a scar. She was actually proud of the scars she had and could tell a vivid story about each. "What does it look like, Skeet?"

"Forget it. You'll be fine."

When they got back to the boat they put the clam basket back into the cool water. Skeeter made sure the burlap was wet enough and placed it over the catch. Skeeter found two pieces of flat drift wood. He put them down on the sand in a spot the sun couldn't see. Jill lugged the heavy box that held their lunch and set it down next to one of the drift wood benches and opened it.

Skeeter watched her take the food out. "You went to a lot of trouble making this lunch."

"I know." Jill said. "But, I wanted to."

They had forgotten about being hungry until they sat down and smelled the salad. With cheeks stuffed full and bulging, they chewed in silence not looking at each other. The girl gobbled her sandwich down faster than Skeeter and after the last bite was swallowed she let fly with a terrific belch, then followed that with a satisfied, "aaaaahhh."

"Good one" Skeeter said sarcastically. "We need to go. It's gettin'hot."

"Swoosh. Swoosh." I sailed past them.

"Whoa." Skeeter belted out.

Out of nowhere it seemed, but, from the tall pines I came. I zoomed past Skeeter's head and flew low along the beach. Then up again, turned west over the bay, I headed back again. This time, I glided past the two of them.

"Rueben. Rueben." They both cheered me on. I was the black dive bomber.

"Cack, cack, cack." I answered, and came to a stop on the bow of the boat.

"Hi boy." Skeeter said. "You hungry?"

I hopped off the boat and walked toward the clammers. Jill loved the fact that a crow followed them around. Even though I cared a great deal for Jill, I was a little wary of her. But, that was OK. She knew I had been around Skeeter since I was born. I trusted Skeeter.

Skeeter watched Jill smile at me. She didn't look like a Jill-o' lantern now. She just looked like his friend.

Jill walked to the boat, rummaged through the lunch box, and found the Mason jar. I flapped my wings and perched on the stern where I could see what she was doing. I cocked my head from left to right so that my left eye could see the basket. I also watched Jill for any sudden movements. A crow always has to be mindful of his surroundings and any danger. Even though I trusted Skeeter I would always remain a bird of the wild.

"There's a little bit of chicken left." Jill shouted in Skeeter's direction. "Here boy you'll like this." Jill tried to get her pointer finger to reach the bottom of the jar but she couldn't quite reach the leftovers. There was a small pine branch lying next to the boat. She picked up a sandy twig, broke it in half, and scraped the two small chunks of chicken onto the wooden seat. She saw the sand stuck to the stick as she poked at the chicken. And, before she could get the stick out of the jar, she had gotten sand on the food. "Dang it," she said. Rueben's a scavenger who's eaten worse stuff than sand. He won't mind. She thought.

I was certainly hungry, but as far as I was concerned, Jill would have to get farther away from it. I couldn't take the chance that she would lunge for me and try to grab me. Even though she had never tried to catch me before, I was not going to be careless. Anyway, I had let Jill rub my head and back many times while I perched on Skeeter's shoulder.

"Go on Rue, eat." Jill put hands on her hips and cocked her head mocking the crow.

"You're standin' too close, Knot Head." Skeeter said looking up from the clam basket.

Jill didn't answer but turned and walked in Skeeter's direction. When it was safe to get the food, I walked from the stern to the top of the boat's side rails then sideways toward the seat. I switched my sight between the friends and the food until I was standing over the chicken. I looked to the right and then behind before I took a quick stab and grabbed a chunk. I held it in my beak a second or two then pointed my head toward the sky, hit it twice with my tongue and let it fall into my craw. Twice more I did this until the chicken was gone. I studied the seat to make sure I had gotten it all. I flapped my wings and jumped back on the stern. After staring at the two of them for a minute, I flapped a few times and took off and headed for a nearby pine. Then, after rubbing my beak clean on the branch, I shot down real fast and zoomed once again past them toward town.

Back over the bay and again, I zoomed by them toward town. "He's telling us its time to get these clams home." Skeeter said.

"Ok. Let's go." She answered and grabbed her wire handle. They put the basket of clams in the boat and Jill arranged the wet burlap.

The "BE-BOP-A-LULA" Kid

Skeeter made sure he had the lunch box and the rest of their stuff in the boat. He untied the boat and they both pushed it along the wet sand until it floated freely.

Jill took her position on the bow and Skeeter, giving it one last shove, climbed in too. Since he was facing backwards Skeeter couldn't actually see her fiddling with her hair. But, he could tell that something was going on. He sensed her weight shifting back and forth and wondered what she was doing. "Dag, nab it." Jill mumbled.

Skeeter stopped rowing and turned to look at her. She was clawing at her hair near her right ear. She pulled her hand away and the gum she had been chewing that morning strung from behind her hair to her fingers. She stuffed the gum in her mouth and tried to pick the rest from behind her ear. "I forgot I parked my gum behind my ear before we ate."

"It's stuck all in your hair. Ha ha." Skeeter pointed at her. "You're about a numb skull. Ha ha ha."

"Yea, like it never happened to you? Who cares anyway? I'll just cut my hair off anyway." Actually, Jill didn't care. She was having fun and school wasn't starting for a long time. She had plenty of time to grow her hair back. "It's not like I'm havin' some fancy picture taken or somethin'."

I heard Skeeter laughing and sailed nearby to see what all the excitement was about. "Caw, caw, cack, cack, cack." I blurted out.

"Ah shut up Rueben." Jill yelled. "I'll feed you some nice sticky gum in a sardine and see how you like it."

That made Skeeter mad as fire. He was starting to get a little tired of her. He rowed harder and the boat lunged ahead making Jill jolt off of her seat.

"Hey. What's with you?" She said.

Skeeter didn't answer but kept rowing. I gotta' get her off of this boat. He thought. He let the boat glide when he got it close to the dock. He reached out and grabbed the edge of a rotting plank. The boat stopped its forward motion. He took the rope and tied it around a cleat. He climbed out and tied another rope from the bow to another cleat. Jill tried to help with the rope, but Skeeter snatched it from under her before she could reach it. He kept busy unloading the rakes and the empty lunch box. She tried to help him with the heavy clam basket but he pushed her hand away and with all his might heaved it onto the pier. Neither one spoke a word.

Skeeter thought about how to get her clams to her house. The lunch box and the clams would be way too heavy for her to carry. He didn't want to push his bike along side of her as she walked home to Peach Street. He hefted the clams into the crate on the back of his bike.

"I need to get the clams on ice. I'll bring yours over later." Skeeter said with no emotion.

"Don't bother." She snipped. "I can take them now." Jill was tired of being around him too.

"Fine." Skeeter said.

Jill snatched up one of the burlap sacks and walked ahead to Skeeter's bike. She found the opening in the top and counted out twenty-four beauties. Gently, she put the clams in the sack. She gathered up the Mason jar and the other picnic tools and put them inside too. She slung the bag over her shoulder and bent forward to offset the weight and marched toward her house.

Skeeter watched her fill the bag and when he knew she was out of hearing range he said out loud, "What a knot head. She didn't even ask if she could use the bag." He watched her struggle with the load until she was out of sight.

Skeeter secured the boat and washed off the mess I had made with the chicken. He kicked sand onto Jill's stupid lunch box as he walked to his trusty bike. "What a jerk." He mumbled. "Want a ride Rueben?" I was back on the boat studying the wet spot that Skeeter had made of my lunch plate.

"Caw, caw." I answered.

Skeeter pushed the kick stand up and balanced his load. "Flap, flap." I leapt up and stood on Skeeter's left shoulder.

"Let's get out of here, Rue."

Skeeter and his truest friend rode along together thinking about how good those clams were going to taste.

CHAPTER 10

The following morning, Skeeter's eyes opened at the usual time. Waiting outside his window, I saw him yawn and stretch his arms toward the ceiling. He thought about what Jill had said to me about feeding me bubble gum and wondered why she had been so mean. He wished his friends were in town so that he'd have somebody else to do stuff with. But, they weren't.

"Good morning, Son." His mother sang when she saw him skip down the kitchen stairs.

"Mornin', Mom"

"You want me to scramble a couple of eggs for breakfast? How about some nice grits?"

"No thanks, I'll just fix some cereal."

"How 'bout some bacon?"

"No thanks."

"What are your plans for today?"

"Probably gonna' go out in my boat and see what I can find. I might go fishin' or somethin.' I need to think about a plan to earn money to see Gene."

"If you can catch a mess of fish, I'll fry 'em up for dinner. If you can catch a couple of those big drum fish, that would be even better." Skeeter's mother stared out the window for a few minutes. "I love drum fish."

"I know, Mom, me too."

"Are you OK Son?"

Skeeter wrinkled his eyebrows and wondered what she meant. "Ma'am?"

"Well, startin' the summer with a broken arm in a cast and having none of your friends around, I'm a little worried about you."

"I have a new friend who just moved here. We've been havin' some fun."

"A new friend? Well, that's nice. What's his name?"

"Don't tell Dad, OK, but my friend's not a he, he's a she. Her name is Jill. Her family rented a house on Peach Street right after school was out." Skeeter said. "But she's really OK. She does everything my friends and I do. She likes to play baseball, and climb trees, and throw rocks, and everything. She always tries to beat me at whatever we do. She can hit a baseball real far and she ain't, I mean, she isn't, scared of anything. She'll pick up frogs and everything. She doesn't even care if spiders crawl on her."

"What's her last name, honey? She must live in the house next to the park. Is that where she lives? I heard a family of men moved in there."

"Yes ma'am, the gray wooden house. I don't know her last name."

"Oh." His mom said.

"What's the matter with that, Mom?" Skeeter asked.

"Nothin' honey. I just heard that they seem kinda' rough. I don't think they're used to much."

"What does that mean?"

"Oh, nothing. Nothing at all. Well, you be nice to them. I know you will anyway."

"Do you mean her family is poor or something'?"

"Well, it doesn't really matter, does it?"

"Not to me," Skeeter said. "I never even talked to a girl before. Except my cousins. They don't really count."

"Why did you say not to tell Dad?"

"Because when I was in the first grade, I told him about this girl named Linda who liked me. He teased me to death about her. I never even looked at her or said one word to her. But he kept teasin' and teasin' me real bad. I don't ever want to talk about another girl around him. So, I don't want to be teased just because a friend happens to be a girl. She ain't even like a girl. And, she wears boys' clothes and everything."

"Boys' clothes?"

"Yes ma'am. I think she is the only girl in the family and she has to wear handy downs from her brothers or somethin'."

"Handy downs?" His mother squinted her eyes like they might be connected to her ears when she heard something weird. "Handy downs?" She said again.

"Yea. You know when somebody gives you stuff they outgrew. Handy downs."

"Oh. Honey, you mean hand-me-downs." Skeeter's mom smiled at him, grabbed both sides of his face and said, "You are the best kid ever."

"Yea, I know." Skeeter said. "You tell me that all the time." Wow, I said something cute, Skeeter thought. I'll have to use that one again, sometime.

Skeeter ate his cereal, wiped his mouth on his napkin, and took the bowl and spoon to the kitchen sink.

"Bye Mom"

"Good bye, Son. Have fun. Be careful."

Skeeter gathered two fishing poles, packed a jar of worms he kept in the dirt under the back steps, and a bucket to put the day's catch in. He hopped on his bike and peddled north on Fig Street toward Kings Creek.

"Caw. Caw. Caw. Cack. Cack." I greeted Skeeter and I glided past the young fisherman.

"You wanna' race me, black bird?" Skeeter yelled. "Let's go, then."

Skeeter put his head down and pushed his feet against the pedals, as hard as he could. Overhead, I flew in circles around him and called out in crow talk. Skeeter just knew that I was laughing at him for being slow.

"Be bop a lula, she's my baby. Be bop a lula, I don't mean maybe. Be bop a lula, she's my baby." Skeeter sang the song all over town.

Enough, all ready, I screamed to myself. Oh no, GENE ATTACK!

At least Skeeter has branched out to sing a verse. "She's the girl with the red blue jeans. She's the queen of all the teens."

We found Jill sitting on the steps under the shade of the Pavilion. She had run from the bay across the burning hot sand and was resting her bare feet on the cool concrete. Once school was out for the summer, no kid in Cape Charles wore shoes again until school started in September. Except, of course, for going to church, you never thought about it. This was an unwritten rule. Even the hardened soles of their summer-time feet couldn't take the heat of the sand for more than a few steps. The Pavilion was the perfect place for them to think.

Elbows on her knees, Jill rested her head in her hands. "How are we gonna' earn enough money to see the Gene show?"

"That'll be a breeze."

"How's that, Mr. Know-It-All?"

"Look. You asked me. Do you want to know or not?"

Jill spit. "That's why I asked, Smart-ass."

"You cuss too much." Skeeter said.

"You're not the boss of me."

"Why would I want to be?"

"Well. There ain't nobody else to be the boss of. Like somebody would let ya'." Jill had the last word.

You know, Bud? Their constant bickering gets to me. They'll be safe enough here for a while. I'm getting out of here and give my ears a rest. I remembered seeing an ice cream vendor earlier on Mason Avenue. Perhaps, I can find a discarded cone with a little cool cream sweetness left inside, without the ants would be best.

Skeeter explained. "This is how we do it. The town has a big celebration for Independence Day that lasts a whole week. We can earn money helping the carnival guys set up rides and games and stuff like that." Skeeter explained.

"What else?" Jill wanted some real excitement and this sounded like the best chance ever. "Is there a snake show or somethin' like that?"

"Well, sometimes they have contests for kids to win stuff."

"Money? Like what kind of contests? Anything I can try?"

"Probably. But it's gonna be hard for you to beat me."

"You're an arrogant jackass." Jill shouted.

She stood up. Skeeter knew he'd better run. He sprang down the steps toward the water. He wasn't thinking about the hot sand now or about the plaster cast on his arm. He had to get in the water first. Jill wasn't strong enough to dunk him except if she caught him by surprise. Skeeter turned his head and saw her gaining on him. "Twelve-year-old cusser!" he yelled.

Jill clenched her jaws together and ground her teeth and sprinted harder.

Skeeter stepped on a jagged edge of an oyster shell that caused him to hop and take a half step. That was all it took for Jill to catch him. Skeeter saw her hand stretched out at him. He tried to go faster but it was too late. He felt her fingers slide inside the elastic waist band of his swimming suit. Then, as she jerked his suit backward, his feet came off the sand and he landed on his stomach at the edge of the water. He was just a few feet from his goal. His face was planted against a glob of sponge sea weed.

"Ah, man." he hollered. "That's the gooiest, nastiest looking, washed up mess I've ever seen. It stinks too."

Jill kept running now. She had to get away and not go in the water. Skeeter could over-power her there, and she surely could come close to drowning, something she wanted no part of. "I'm thirteen, Clyde!" She shouted.

They both had forgotten about the cast. He couldn't get it wet. It would get soft and melt away.

Jill ran up the beach hooting with laughter.

Skeeter wiped the goo off his face and walked, knee high, into the cool bay. Using his good hand, he washed the decaying mush off his skin, back into the salt water.

Skeeter shook his head a little and smiled.

"What a jerk," he muttered.

Jill ran until she was out of sight. She continued the three blocks to Peach Street. "What kind of contests is he talking about? She asked out loud.

CHAPTER 11

Maybe it was because he had gotten another year older, but Skeeter felt more excited about the town's celebration of Independence Day than any year he could remember. Everything looked a little different this year. The Ferris wheel, the carousel, and the other rides were the same, but this year the children seemed younger, and the teenagers seemed older.

Cape Charles hummed with excited activity. The July 4th celebration was a week away. Skeeter wasn't sure who would be in town the whole week. The kids who were in town, the ones who didn't have regular jobs, all turned out at "the hump" every day and each was hoping to earn some extra money.

"The hump" is a huge pile of dirt with a hard surfaced road on top. It's either an overpass or an underpass. I never could get that straight. Anyway, the road on top lets cars and trucks drive from one side of the railroad tracks to the other and the tracks go underneath. Between "the hump" and the bay is a big open space where the carnival rides and midway set up.

There were the usual games of skill. A rifle shooting gallery, ring toss games, a basketball shooting booth, a booth to knock stuffed cats off a shelf, a baseball throwing booth, and food vendors lined up in miniature streets. It was a kids' paradise. It was a place where every kid had a chance to win a stuffed animal, and a bigger chance to lose all his money. I was as excited as Skeeter. Seven more days, how could we wait that long?

"Wenus. Did you see the booth with the mummified arm?" Skeeter yelled.

"What?" Wenus asked.

"Yea. For fifty cents you can go in and see this old dead arm of some cannibal guy."

Wenus's eyes bugged out like a stomped on toad frog. "Cool."

"I don't know if I'm gonna do it. I need to earn money for my Gene Vincent ticket, not spend money." Skeeter told him.

Wenus patted his wallet in his back pocket. "I got some birthday money saved. I'm gonna' have some fun with it." He told Skeeter.

"Why don't you get your head read? I don't know, though. They may charge you double." Wenus teased Skeeter.

"Hardy, har." Then Skeeter thought about a saying he heard his mother say; "There's a lot of truth in a joke." "What are you talkin' about?" Skeeter asked.

"A gypsy lady feels your head and stuff."

Skeeter did a Gene move. "Your stuff?"

"No. I mean she feels the bumps on a person's head and tells the person about his future. You know, a fortune teller lady."

I saw Skeeter's eyes widen with interest. Oh, the things he would like to know.

"I wonder if the lady can tell me if I'm really gonna' get to see Gene."

"Do it." Wenus said. "I'd like to see that."

Skeeter started walking. "You ain't gonna' see nothin.' See ya." Skeeter was on a mission to find the fortune teller. Of course, I knew where she was. I flew ahead of him. He followed me around the maze of the temporary city.

"I see it Rue." Skeeter shouted. There were six or so wooden frames, maybe ten feet tall and fifteen feet wide. Canvas was stretched across the frames. Painted on the canvas panels in bright colors were pictures of long stemmed roses and gypsy women's heads.

Across the top panel, in big block letters, the word PHRENOLOGY was painted. There was an opening into the tent with curtains across it to close the inside off from view. I suppose this was done when a person was getting the actual head feeling.

Down the left side of the front panel was painted, COME IN AND HAVE YOUR HEAD READ. YOUR HEAD IS LIKE AN OPEN BOOK TO US. SPEAKS DIFFERENT LANGUAGES. Down the other panel it said, SHE WILL TELL YOU WHAT YOU WANT TO KNOW ABOUT LOVE, MARRIAGE, BUSINESS, AND TROUBLE.

I clawed Skeeter's shoulder as he stood in front of the booth. "Wow. This is great Rueben. I need to know if I'll get to see Gene. Let's go, now. I need to make some money. We'll come back later."

I took off then and circled the entire carnival area. I kept Skeeter in sight as usual. I watched him shuffle along Mason Avenue. Oh no. "GENE ATTACK!" Ah, ha, ha. Poor boy, I'm glad no one saw him but me.

After the momentary attack, Skeeter composed himself and hopped up the stairs of the Northampton Hotel. I watched him pull the screen door open and let himself inside. I cocked my head toward "the hump" and spied the Ferris wheel. Since I'd never seen one before, I flew to the top and perched on the highest part. It was now the tallest building in town. It was a spectacular view of the town and beyond. From here, I could spy on everyone without having to concentrate on flying. This may come in handy.

Skeeter came out of the hotel carrying a large cardboard box. He set the box down, then disappeared around the corner. Shadrack had called his name. Shortly, they appeared with an extension ladder. I flew closer and glided to the grass near the sidewalk.

"This is gonna' take all day." Wenus scratched his head and looked up at the side of the building. "I'm scared of heights."

"Don't worry, I'll climb the ladder. You just keep the tools ready." Skeeter was the boss of this outfit.

"Yes Boss," Shadrack said sarcastically.

The boys opened the first of ten similar boxes. Each box held bright red, white, and blue striped cloth. There was one for each window of the hotel and they were made to hang below each window sill. There were miles of ribbon too, that they would weave through the porch rails.

"This place is gonna look great." Skeeter said, smiling at his "men."

Two hours later, when the work was over and the decorating was complete, Skeeter paid his helpers and kept $5.00 for himself.

CHAPTER 12

Later, when the sun had sunk behind the bay, Skeeter sat on a bench and started planning. I glided down and stood next to him. "Want a peanut, Rue?" Skeeter tossed a nut in my direction. I studied it a bit. Blue lint from his pocket stuck to it. I snapped it into smaller pieces and somehow the lint fell off of it.

"You gonna' do it?" Jill asked, pressing her fingertips to the top of her head. She dragged herself toward us. Her skinny legs were caked with dirt and they had a layer of dust on top of the dirt. She had a dirt splotch around her mouth where a bubble she had blown earlier stuck to her face.

Skeeter chuckled at the dirt ring. "You think I should?"

"Hel….heck yea. You have to. You have enough money don't ya'?"

"Yea." Skeeter hesitated.

"Ya' scared, Mr. Teen Idol?" She teased.

"No. What's with you?"

Jill spit on the ground next to his feet. "Nothin'. I'm just messin' with ya." She grinned.

"Let's go then. I'll show you I'm not scared. You see any dead people coming out because they got their heads squeezed too hard and their temples got mashed in? That causes instant death, ya' know."

"What does?"

Skeeter looked at her like she was the dumbest person ever. "If you hit a baby in the temple, it causes instant death. Just like drinkin' pee."

"What?" Jill's upper lip wrinkled her nose and pushed it up almost between her eyes.

"Haven't you been taught not to mess with a baby's temples because their brains are right under their skin?"

Jill put her hands on her hips. "Yea, but what does pee have to do with it?"

"Well. Pee is deathly poisonous and if you drink it, it causes instant death."

"Who says?"

Skeeter stabbed at his chest with his finger. "My Dad."

"Really? That's what he told you?"

Uh-oh. Jill was approaching no-man's land now. To a kid, questioning the wisdom of a friend's dad was strictly forbidden.

"Oh." Jill said in a quieter voice. "Who would drink pee anyway?"

Skeeter got a dumb look on his face. "I don't know. Let's go."

Jill stopped Skeeter with a straight arm across his ribs. "Wait. I'm gettin' ice cream."

Now Bud, here's an opportunity to get my fill of ice cream. When these two handle ice cream, some of it is going to hit the ground. Ha, ha. Then it's mine.

Skeeter and I watched Jill pull a coin out from her shorts pocket. The three of us faced a faded white aluminum camper that was converted into an open air rolling sugar emporium. The sign's green and yellow letters proclaimed, ICE CREAM NOVELTIES. What kid wouldn't gravitate toward an ice cream stand in the middle of a southern July?

"What cha' want Skinny?" Porky Simmons, a tenth grader who lived outside of town, was leaning his large self out the service window. He had on a blue plastic bow tie and his 300 lb. father's white church shirt.

Jill's voice got a high pitch to it as she stuck her head in the ice cream booth, forcing Porky back inside. She shook her fist close to his red nose. Porky was immediately sorry for calling Jill a name. When she turned around and headed toward us, she was holding her coin purse and a double dip cone, too. Her lips were outlined with vanilla.

Skeeter pointed at her and laughed. "You got ice cream on the tip of your nose."

Jill collected the nose cream with the tip of her finger and flicked it at Skeeter. "You want it? Here." Her shot scored a bull's eye by landing perfectly between Skeeter's eyes.

"Take a bite." Jill held the cone out to Skeeter. She had bitten off the top of the semi frozen delight. The sugar cone was already soggy. She held it to Skeeter's mouth, not wanting him to take possession of it. He bit off the next layer. They faced each other. Jill opened her mouth, shoved the cream toward her front teeth and wagged her tongue at Skeeter while she chewed it. Skeeter opened his mouth at her and showed her his mouthful too. They laughed like a couple of idiots with the white cream running from the sides of their mouths and dripping off their chins.

It had to happen soon. My stomach was growling and I could taste that ice cream now. I couldn't wait for the cone to fall to the ground. Once it happened, I could join the feast. It took about ten seconds of insane laughter and the cone was mine. While I took my fill of the treat, they wiped their mouths on their shirt sleeves and walked toward the fortune teller again.

"Sit." Skeeter pushed Jill toward a wooden vegetable crate.

"What?"

"I want to figure out what to say. You know. What to ask about."

"Find out if you're gonna' be able to go to the Gene Show."

"You think I should just ask her outright?" Skeeter licked ice cream off his lips.

"Yes, Goof."

The sun sank into the bay and the carnival took on a life of its own. The festive lights of the signs and attractions proclaimed the regalia of the celebration. The roar of the monstrous electricity generators, that seemed so loud during the heat of the day now blended into the sounds of people screaming with excitement in the cool night air.

Now, who better than a crow, knows when it's truly dark? I mean "midnight" dark. I can feel it. I can see it. I can taste it. Jill and Skeeter knew when it was dark enough to have a fortune told, too. Dark clouds slid in front of the moon stealing the moon's glow. A cool breeze caused the temperature to drop. The time was right.

"Think its dark enough now for the fortune teller to work her strongest powers?" Jill's eyes expressed her growing anticipation of the magic of which Skeeter would soon be the victim.

Skeeter was in mental preparation. "It's time. Rueben, you'd better not be seen by the gypsies. They're not too fond of your kind." He said to me without looking in my direction.

"And if they see you with us, they might not let Skeeter go in." Jill added. "They might think we are all bad luck."

"The fortune teller may even cast a spell on me so I won't get to ever see Gene." Skeeter said.

I saw the perfect perch. It was directly across from the psychic's tent and high above any direct light.

"Whoosh, whoosh." I flapped my wings and lifted myself into a warm summer breeze. The perfect perch, indeed, I had sight of the booth and the kids.

Skeeter and Jill studied the tent. Jill nudged him with her shoulder. "Go."

A gypsy man looked the two up and down. "I want to know my future." Skeeter's voice squeaked with fear. Jill snickered.

Chapter 12

"How much money you got?" The gypsy snarled in a deep voice.

"I have….."

Jill yanked Skeeter's arm and gave him a wide eyed stare. "How much does it cost to have a person's head read? Is it based on head size?" Jill interrupted her bumbling friend.

"No. It is based on what I say is how much you can pay." They could barely understand his broken English.

"I have one dollar to spend." Skeeter stepped in front of Jill.

"That's all?"

Skeeter didn't answer.

"OK. One dollar it is."

I watched Skeeter shove his hand down deep in a front pants pocket, pull out a crumpled dollar and hand it to the man.

"It will be just one few minutes more." The gypsy relieved Skeeter of his dollar.

The canvas panel jerked open with the screech of metal curtain rings sliding across the steel cable. A lady we didn't recognize stood in the dark opening holding a handkerchief. She sniffed a few times, blotted her nose, then each eye.

"Holy crap." Jill whispered.

"I wonder what happened to her." Skeeter whispered back. "Maybe they're happy tears."

"Nah. She's cryin'."

"Thank you Madam Zelda. It's very clear to me now." The lady blew her nose into her hanky.

"You're welcome, Sweetheart. It will all work out as I have told you so."

As the lady turned, she brushed her leg against the rough canvas of the tent. "Whaaa…" She started sobbing.

Jill pointed to the lady's leg. The canvas had ripped her stockings and they were tearing all the way up and under her dress. "She's not havin' fun." Jill mumbled.

The fortune teller scanned the crowd. "Now, who is next to having his fortune told?"

Madam Zelda's oversized silver hoops stretched her ear lobes. She smiled at her next customers. One of her front teeth was black with rot. It was next to a gold tooth that sparkled in the bright light that illuminated the tent's entrance.

"I think I am." Skeeter squeaked again.

She stared at each of them and commanded. "Come then."

I dropped from my hiding place and flew to a branch behind the tent. I kept swift and silent as I glided from the branch to the grass. I walked toward a soft beam of light that escaped through the tent where a side and back canvas came together. That's where I stood to get a view of the procedure.

A table, built low to the ground, was in the center of the musty smelling room. I could almost see the odor escaping, it was so strong. Anyway, the table had gold fabric fringe hanging from all four sides. The top was covered with floor tile. The tiles were hand painted with a street scene of several buildings. There were other objects painted on the tabletop to look like they were real. Three dimensional, I believe, is what they call it. A paper clip, a lady's ring, and some playing cards, each looked real as real could be.

Each corner of the table top had an electrical light socket with a tiny bulb. They were barely burning and put out very little light. On one wall of the canvas tent was painted a silhouette of the human head, all in white. Black lines were painted on the head creating different sections, each having a different name.

TRUTH   DESTINY   LOVE
PASSION   FIDELITY   MONEY

The mystic gestured toward a straight backed wooden chair facing the table. "Sit in the tall chair." Skeeter obeyed. Now pointing at Jill she said. "You. You sit on the boy's left facing the table of truth."

Jill's upper lip curled toward her nose when the musk of the dank room found her. She looked at Skeeter as she lowered herself onto a short wooden stool. His nose imitated hers as he caught wind of the odor too.

The fortune teller turned her back to them. She limped when she walked away, disappearing into a dark corner of the tent. The crack of a match against the rough side of the match box cut the silence and startled them. As the flame moved about in the hands of the woman, the smell of incense mixed with the rotten funk that choked them.

"Jeez." Skeeter whispered. "That stinks so bad."

"Shhhh. Don't remind me."

"What's passion?" Skeeter pointed to the big white head and squiggly part of the divided brain on the chart.

"I think it's kissin' and stuff." Jill squinted her eyes trying to make out the image on the head.

Her knobby hands completely covered Skeeter's scalp. "Keep still now while Madam Zelda feels the bumps on your head." He was getting a huge knot in his throat. Her fingertips danced through his short hair. They stopped occasionally to squeeze something she believed would tell her what was in his future.

Jill started swallowing every ten seconds or so. On her upper lip, sweat glistened in the dim light. She swallowed again and again.

Skeeter broke the eerie silence by blurting out. "I have to know if I will get to see the great Gene Vincent perform in Norfolk at the end of the summer."

"Silence." The sage shouted at him. Her hands moved over the top of the Table of Truth. I got as close to them as I could, but stayed just outside the tent.

Jill thought if she could burp she'd be OK. She kept swallowing and sweating.

The gypsy stood behind Skeeter. The four lights began to glow brighter.

I'm gonna do it. Jill thought. I'm gonna' burp.

She concentrated on trying to burp. Skeeter could barely stand the stench much longer. As Jill's eyes wondered across the table where the Gypsy's hand had been, she saw something she wasn't prepared for. On the table just above the painted cards was the dried up foot of a chicken. Below that was a monkey's foot. Both dead. And they were pointed at her.

Then it happened. Jill burped. It was silent but ugly. Skeeter looked down, away from the table. He realized why the gypsy limped. Her big right toe had been cut off and her foot wasn't healed up yet. He felt ill, really ill. Glancing over at his friend, his eyes passed over the dead feet. His stomach churned. He hoped seeing Jill would calm him down. She was no help. He saw her face was white as chalk.

Jill's eyes were watery and glazed over. There on her now pale freckled face, oozing from the corners of her mouth, what had been delicious cool ice cream was now pink smelly vomit.

Skeeter watched it drip from her chin and he knew they had to get out before they gagged to death. Now, I was feeling sick, too. I had to help them. I bolted through the opening in the canvas, flapped my wings as loud as I could and lit in the center of the Table of Truth.

The soothsayer screeched and screamed and lunged for a broom near the doorway. Skeeter's chair tipped over backward, spilling him to the trampled grass. Jill fell off her stool and spit out a mouthful of sour burped up ice cream.

"Let's go." Skeeter yelled.

They crawled on all fours until they could stand up and run. I saw the nine toed woman scurrying around with the broom. She was headed back into the tent. What was on her mind was a dead crow. Speaking in tongues, only gibberish spewed from her blood red lips. "Get out. I'll kill you. You, black wizard, will ruin our lives. I know all answers, not you. You are trash, a rat with wings. Scavenger. I know all! Not you!"

I tucked my wings in, tight to my sides. I scurried through the canvas curtains and past my previous hiding place.

"Thud! Whomp!" The broom beat at the ground inches from my tail feathers.

Once clear of the tent, I flew up to the branch where I'd watched the kids enter the booth. There was no sign of them. I wondered where they could be. Where could they go and not be seen? I know.

The cool salt air cleared their senses, but not the taste in their mouths. Without stopping, they had run the four blocks to the ally where they'd first met. Gasping and panting, they stood, bent over with their hands on their knees. Jill spit about a hundred times trying to get the taste out of her mouth. Throw up had shot out of her nose too.

Skeeter looked at her and spit on the grass. "That's the worst thing I've ever done."

"Me too." Jill gasped for clean air.

I frantically flew to the alley hoping they'd gone there. I let out a welcoming "Cack" and glided to a window sill at eye level.

"Thanks, Rue." Skeeter said.

Chapter 12

"You saved our lives." Jill praised me.

Skeeter blew out a breath then sniffed in her direction. "You don't smell so good."

Jill looked down and saw vomit matted in her shirt. "Sorry. I've had enough for one day.

I took to the carnival sky and sailed around in circles to stretch my wings. Skeeter and Jill left the alley and walked away from the carnival. When they got to Peach Street, Jill turned north to her house.

"See ya'." She called out.

Skeeter kicked an empty soda can. "Bye."

CHAPTER 13

"Son? The mail came. There's a letter for you on the hall table." Skeeter's mom said.

Skeeter bounded to the front hall and picked up the white envelope. It was postmarked August 3, 1956

"It's August, already?" He asked me through the screened door. "Summer's almost over. I can't believe it."

He studied the address:

Master Llewellyn Whitmel
888 Monroe Avenue
Cape Charles, Virginia

"I must be in trouble."

"Why do you think that, Honey?" His mother asked.

"Nobody ever uses my real name except at the beginning of the school year and on report cards." Skeeter said.

Oh, no. Report cards? Not in the middle of summer. There's nothin' to report. Skeeter didn't like this already. He didn't bother looking at the return address. He tore open the flap and pulled on the thick paper inside. Out came a folded card with a drawing of kids dancing at a party.

Oh, no. He thought. He flipped the card open and read:

Your Presence is Requested to Attend the First Annual
Cape Charles Autumn Dance
To Be Held on Saturday Evening, August 18, 1956

In The Cafeteria of Cape Charles School
The Festivities Will Begin at 7:00 PM and End at 9:30 PM
Gentlemen Guests Will Be Wearing Coats and Ties
Misses Will Be Wearing Party Dresses
R.S.V.P.

Skeeter dropped his hand to his side, barely holding the card. He looked at the wood floor below.

"This is bad, real bad." He said. "I'm not goin'.' I ain't goin'."

Skeeter knew Wenus, Shadrack, and Peanut wouldn't go either. "That's it then. No big deal. There's no way I'm goin' to a stupid dance." Skeeter had made up his mind.

Leaving the invitation to boredom on the table, Skeeter passed through the kitchen and out the back door. Why do grown-ups have to bother kids during summer vacation? Skeeter thought. A dance. Jeez? Holy cow. What could be fun about wasting a perfectly good Saturday night wearing church clothes, and watchin' a bunch of girls gigglin' like crazy and telling each other how beautiful they all look? Plus, it was the last Saturday night before school started. And, it's almost four weeks away, so you have to keep worryin' about it too. This summer is getting ruined real fast. And, no teacher knows about rock'n'roll and any teacher who does isn't gonna let kids play rock'n'roll music.

This is a major disaster. His head pounded. Wait a minute. It would be a disaster. But, I ain't goin'. So forget about it. It ain't gonna' happen.

Skeeter was now on the porch with me. "I'm goin' to the doctor's office now, Mom. Come on, Rue, let's go get this cast off."

I flew overhead as he peddled the two blocks to Dr. Griffith's office.

CHAPTER 14

The two weeks after Skeeter got his cast off were the fastest two weeks of the summer. Skeeter's arm gradually got back to normal. After many ball field discussions, everyone agreed that going to the big dance would be something they could all make fun of. Each decided to go. Tonight was the big night. Skeeter's house was a buzz.

"Make sure you have a clean handkerchief." Skeeter's dad said.

"What for, Dad?"

"In case you have to blow your nose. Or, you might have to lend it to a girl so she can clean something or cry in it or something."

"Well, I won't be lending it to any girl. If a girl needs it that bad, she can just have it."

His mother looked proud. "Use your best manners, Honey. I know that you'll be the most handsome young man there."

"Ah, Mom. I won't be the most handsome kid there." Actually, Skeeter was admiring himself in the hall mirror as he spoke. He had put on his best "foo foo" water, shined his church shoes, and brushed his teeth. For someone who wanted no parts of this dance, I couldn't understand what changed his mind. He glanced in the mirror one last time and patted his pants pocket making sure his knife was there.

"Bye." Skeeter scooted out the front door. "You comin', Rue? I got a clean booger vault. I'm as ready as I'll ever be."

"Cack, Cack." I was excited too. I quite enjoyed this night life business. Much easier for me to spy on humans, you know.

On the sidewalk in front of Skeeter's house, Shad and Peanut waited for him. Shad had some sort of shiny grease in his hair.

"Hey there, Llewellyn."

"Shadradicus!" Skeeter yelled back.

"You feel the Gene attack comin' on anytime soon?"

"Shaddup." Skeeter sneered.

"You do it so good, buddy. You melt all the girls. I mean turn 'em to jelly."

"Aw shut up." Skeeter said.

Shadrack broke into a hilarious imitation of Skeeter's now famous "Gene Attack."

"Go cat. Go Skeeter, go. Ah, ah, ah." It was Peanut now, just up ahead.

Skeeter answered in his direction. "You can shut up too."

Skeeter's dad walked onto the front porch. "Hey boys, come here for a minute."

"Hi, Mr. Whitmel." Each of the boys answered.

"What's wrong, Dad?"

"Nothing's wrong. I just wanted to tell you some-thing. I know you guys think that you are hep cats and cool guys."

Oh, no. Skeeter thought. Not another lecture.

"I just want each of you to think about something. There'll be girls there tonight who probably aren't as pretty as some others. There'll be shy ones and some, maybe will be a little overweight."

Skeeter looked off into the sky. This is so painful. He thought.

"I want to tell you that the real cool guys, the real men, will ask each of these girls to dance. Think how you'd feel if you went to a dance and no one asked you to join in the fun and dance. How terrible would you feel? If each of you would ask a wall flower girl to dance, just once, you will be someone they'll always remember. Each girl will go home and tell their families that they got asked to dance and they had a good time."

"Oh, no." Skeeter whispered. "These guys will never forgive me for this. This is brutal. Please stop, Dad." Skeeter wanted to disappear.

"Do you understand what I'm saying?" Skeeter's dad was driving it home hard.

"Yes, Mr. Whitmel." Each of them chimed in.

Skeeter's dad stood with his hands on his hips and a stern look on his face like he just delivered the Gettysburg Address. "Ok, then. Now get going and have a good time."

The boys turned toward the now dreaded cotillion. You'd think they were in a fast walking contest. A half a block later, Skeeter turned to look back. "We understand,

Dad." Skeeter paused then yelled, "but, it ain't gonna' happen!"

They ran another block then slowed to a walk. "What are we gonna' do at this shindig anyway?" Peanut asked the other boys.

"I dunno. We're supposed to be all polite and crap and learn how to be adults. I even had to bring a clean snot rag." Skeeter said.

"Me, too." Peanut said.

"Same here." Shadrack was in too. "If there's a lot of snottin' going on we'll be ready." Shad thought for a minute. "I'm not sure girls have snot."

"Oh yes, they do." Skeeter said. "I threw Jill down in the surf so hard she sucked in so much bay water that when she hacked it up a big wad of snot blew out her nose and landed on my leg."

"Gross." They all agreed.

Shad was in hysterics. "I don't know if a lot of snotin' will be goin' on but, if Skeet does the Gene, there'll probably be some pants peein' too."

Skeeter couldn't hold it in any longer and even he laughed at that one. "I ain't cleanin' up no pee with my hanky."

Peanut asked Skeeter. "You gonna' dance with your girlfriend all night?"

"Who?" Skeeter looked puzzled.

"You." Peanut said.

"I know me, jackass. What girlfriend?"

"Jill. Who else could I mean?"

"Jill? She ain't my girlfriend. I never even think about her bein' a girl, anyway. She can do anything we can do. She plays ball as good as you, Peanut. And, she can beat you at arm wrestlin', Shad."

"Yea, I guess you're right. It's just as well. She's a carpenter's dream anyway." Shadrack said.

"What's that suppose to mean?" Skeeter got a little touchy.

"She's a carpenter's dream. She's flat as a board. Ah, ha, ha."

Peanut laughed as loud as Shadrack. "She's a pirate's dream, too." Peanut added.

"A pirate's dream?" Shadrack asked.

"Yea. She's got a sunken chest. Ah, ah, ha, ha." Shadrack and Peanut fell all over each other laughing. "What's with you, Llewellyn? You too good to laugh?"

"No." Skeeter looked at both of them. "That's not funny."

"Sure it's funny, Mr. Goody Two Shoes." Peanut teased him.

It was a good thing Skeeter's hands were stuffed deep into his pants pockets as he rolled them into fists. "She can't help the way she looks." He snapped back.

"Yea? Well you make fun of my big feet and Wenus' red hair and actually, you think you're better than everybody else, anyway." Peanut put Skeeter in his place.

"Look, she's no different lookin' than any other girl in our class." Skeeter said.

Chapter 14

"Back off, Homer." Peanut said to Skeeter. "It was just a joke. I like her fine. She's fun. It was just a joke."

"Get lost." Skeeter said to them. "I forgot somethin'. I'll be there in a little while." Skeeter stopped walking with them and turned toward home. Their laughter and talking got louder as they were joined by other kids along the way. Skeeter walked far enough to be hidden from their view.

"Cack."

"Thanks for bein' a real friend, Rue. Maybe they're right. Maybe I do act like I'm better'n everybody else. I don't mean to." Skeeter felt sorry for himself. I wanted him to get going and stop moping around.

"Cack, cack." I flapped my wings and walked in front of him.

"OK, boy. Let's go."

CHAPTER 15

Jill's house was no buzz. She had never gotten ready for a dance before, much less by herself. Of course, her father and brothers helped her when she was small. But, she was thirteen now and they had no clue how to help a teenage girl do anything.

She studied her reflection in the bathroom mirror. "There sure ain't much to work with." She told the kid who looked back at her. "Momma could make me look purdy."

She took the only dress she had from the tiny closet in her room. She'd outgrown her school clothes from last year and her father couldn't fit all their stuff in the truck and in the car they drove from Lee County. The plan was to see what the Cape Charles girls were expected to wear to school then match Jill up with some new clothes.

Since that had not yet happened, the dress for all occasions would have to do. She wished she had planned for this days ago, but she hadn't, and it was too late now. She had taken a bath and put on clean underwear. Putting on make-up wasn't a problem since there wasn't any in the house and she didn't know what to do with it if she had it. At least I can be clean, she thought.

She had washed her hair and combed it out straight like she usually wore it. She combed her bangs, found some paper cutting scissors, the kind kids use in school, the kind with no points. As best she could, she trimmed her bangs straight across. She snipped some wild sprigs where her hair stopped at the nape of her neck.

"That's the best I can do, Jill," she said to the mirror.

During the snipping, she noticed her finger nails were broken and jagged. Trimming the nails on her right hand was the most awkward thing she had ever attempted. The pre-school scissors added to her frustration. She decided not to attempt her toes since they would be hidden in a pair of white socks. The pressing iron got left behind too so what wrinkles were in her dress would accompany her to the dance. She stared at herself and attempted a smile.

"Holy crap." She said out loud. "What is that?"

She watched her tongue try to squeeze between her two front teeth. There was a piece of dark green spinach caught between them.

"That's nasty lookin'." She said. She jammed the bristles of her tooth brush between them. From behind her teeth, she pushed the brush hard and saw the green glob go air born. It must have stuck to something somewhere because she never saw it land.

When the dress was hanging on her boney frame, she put on her socks and white leather sandals. In the mir-ror, she watched her lip curl up. Something smelled a little funny. It was her dress. It had been cooped up for a while and wasn't exactly fresh.

From the medicine cabinet in the bathroom, she found her family's (since her father and brothers all used it) bottle of Old Spice after shave lotion. She sprinkled a few drops in her hand. Then, to make it her own, she added an equal portion of Dad's fancy smelling Aqua Velva.

It felt cold and tingly on her neck. She rubbed some on the insides of her wrists as she saw a lady do in the drug store. For a second, she didn't know what to do with the rest of it. Not wanting to waste the fragrance on a bath towel, she hoisted up her dress and dried her hands on her underpants.

She spoke out loud. "What about nail polish? I need fingernail polish." Jill bolted down the stairs and found her brother's plastic ship model supplies. She took out a small glass bottle of red paint and a brush. Ten minutes later her fingernails were Candy Apple Red. Twenty minutes after that, she had Candy Apple Red smudges on each side of her dress.

One last look in the mirror, "done" she said. Then just as quickly, "not done," blurted out. "I don't want to do this. I hate bein' a girl. I ain't purdy. I can't dance. This ain't me and I just wanna' be me."

Jill shuffled back to her room and fell across her bed. Through all of this transformation from the old Jill to the, well, same old Jill, I had spied on her. I thought it best to make my presence known. Maybe she'd snap out of her blue funk. I dropped from the tree to the tin covered porch roof. I tried to land hard and make my toe nails tap as loudly as I could. As soon as I hit the roof, Jill's head popped up off the bed and turned to my direction.

"Hi, Rue." She said with a distinct lack of excitement. She did, however, get up and drag herself to the window and sat on the floor. "You're lucky you don't have to wear a dress and dance and act like somebody you're not."

Well Bud, and you too Jilly, that was exactly what I was about to do, except for wearing a dress.

It was all I could do not to 'Cack' in her face. I played it cool to let her talk it out.

Jill grumbled. "I can't dance, anyway."

This girl needs some help, I thought. I walked around a bit, thinking. First, I walked in a straight line down to the end of the porch where she couldn't see me. Then, I marched past her to the other end. On the third pass, I jerked my head in her direction, but kept marching. I made my turn again and made my forth pass. This time, I jerked my head to the right as I got to her and stared at her as I passed. My next pass, I got in front of her and spread my wings half open then stopped, took then two more steps. Then I turned and took two more steps. Each time I turned and stepped, I shook my tail feathers like mad.

Jill was laughing out loud now. "You dancin' for me Rueben? Go bird. Do the jitterbug."

Something possessed me. I was a dancing fool. Jill's laughter was music to me. I jitterbugged as frantically as I could. I did anything to take her mind off herself. I even tried to duplicate Skeeter's Gene. But, with no arms or hips, that was impossible.

Jill got the message, gathered up her purse, and came out the front door. I flew around her in big circles as we crossed the playground to the scene of the cotillion. The overgrown grass rubbed the toes of her sandals and stained the white leather a bright green. She didn't notice nor would she have cared. There was no wind moving the leaves of the town's crepe myrtles. The setting sun streaked the summer sky. Crimson and orange, and yellow and pink, painted a beautiful backdrop for the scene of their first dress up dance.

It wouldn't all be so pretty.

CHAPTER 16

Just inside the doorway of the cotillion ballroom, actually the school gym, stood Willie T, smiling like a proud poppa.

"Mr. Llewellyn Whitmel. My, my. Don't you look handsome as a new mule?"

Willie T was the school's janitor as long as Skeeter could remember. He had known Skeeter's father since before Skeeter was born.

Skeeter smiled and held out his hand. They shook hands every time they met. And, with each shake, they affirmed their mutual respect. Skeeter would often stay after school to talk to Willie. He helped him move desks or set up tables or sweep the floors of the long hallways. Skeeter liked hearing about Willie T's adventures and the funny ways he told stories.

"Tell the truth." Skeeter said.

"And, may the Lord love ya." Willie T answered.

I heard them greet each other this way a million times.

"Thanks Willie. You look pretty good yourself."

"I sure am lookin' forward to seein' you do that Gene thing, I be hearin' about."

"Jeez. How do you know about that?"

"Now, Mr. Whitmel. You know here in Cape Charles, your money's your own, but your business is everybody else's. Ha, ha, ha."

"Yea, yea. I know. Thanks for the help puttin' up the tables and chairs. Why are you still here?"

Willie T got a toothy grin. "I wanted to see you and the other young people at y'all's first dress up dance. I feel like all y'all are my young 'uns."

"Have you seen Jill, the new girl? She lives on Peach near the playground."

"I seen a girl peekin' in the windahs, but she never came in."

Skeeter stuck his nose in the air, squinted, and sniffed. "Somethin' smells bad. Really strange, bad." He sniffed again.

Willie T cut his eyes at Skeeter. "It ain't but so bad though, is it?" He had a goofy looking smile this time. It was a smile that barely showed his front teeth. Even the gold tooth, just left of center was only partially visible. He looked like he had just gotten caught doing something bad.

"Yea. It smells like the science storage room." Skeeter looked around and sniffed again.

Willie T put his hand to his mouth. "Oh, Lawd. I guess it's me then. It ain't no science room."

"Whaddaya mean?"

"I wanted to be wearin' nice clothes tonight too. So, my cousin, see, he works over to the funeral home in Cheriton. He lended me this suit. I gotta' git it back over there tonight 'cause they havin a viewin' in the mornin'. What you smell is embalmin' fluid, I s'pose."

Skeeter stepped back and with huge eyes said. "You mean a dead man wore that suit before?"

"Yyeesss, Lawd. Lots of 'em. Don't tell nobody now, 'cause some people think the suit be hainted. It don't bother me none."

"Good luck gettin' it back on time, Willie" Skeeter moved on.

"Yes sir. You have some fun now. And make sure you dance with all the girls."

"Come on now, Willie T, they'll be linin' up any minute now." Skeeter swaggered toward the front of the school.

"Tell your daddy Willie T said hello."

Something caught Willie T's eye through the wired glass of the gym doors. It was Jill with her hands cupped around her face. Willie T pushed the adjoining door open faster than Jill could react. "Why you standin' there foggin' up my windah glass?"

The odor of embalming fluid and stale gym air made Jill jolt.

"Besides, there's a handsome gentleman headed out the front. I think he's lookin' for you. You the new girl, ain't cha?"

"I guess." Jill said.

"Then git." Willy T closed the door and laughed. "Lawd have mercy. Lawd have mercy. Skeeter done got him a girl friend. She's a skinny thing, too. Ha, ha, ha. Yyeeesss, Lawd."

CHAPTER 17

Skeeter heard Jill before he saw her. "Now, git?" She said out loud. "Who does he think he's talkin' to?" She appeared from the dark side of the school building. Skeeter waited in front.

"Who are you talkin' to?" He said.

"Some man ran me away from the back doors. I was tryin' to see if you were inside."

Skeeter looked at Jill. She was standing in the middle of her only dress. Candy apple red paint was smeared on each side of her dress, near her hips. She looked like a mystery person to him. His best friend was in a dress and was wearing girls' shoes, too. She also wore the tiniest of smiles. She looked nothing like the Jill he knew. Is it even Jill? He wondered for a second or two.

I studied this moment and jumped to a crepe myrtle where I could hear better. Skeeter stood, frozen when he saw her. His mouth opened and he started to speak. Please, Skeeter. Please say something nice. Please tell her how nice she looks. Please give her some sign of approval that you know she's a girl. I pleaded inside.

Then it happened. Skeeter smiled back at her and I heard him. "Look at you."

I was getting nervous. Yes. Come on Skeeter. Tell her. Let her know she's a pretty girl, or any kind of a girl. Say something nice.

Then I heard it, along with Jill. I nearly lost my grip on the branch. "Look at you, a boy in a dress." Skeeter even pointed his finger at her. "You look kinda' silly."

Jill stopped smiling and her pretty eyes looked at her grass stained sandals. "Thanks for not letting me down." She raised her eyes up to meet his.

"Wait. Wait, I didn't mean…"

I saw the panic in Skeeter's eyes, but I believed he still didn't get it. He knew he was in trouble.

Jill looked at him, shook her head and smiled. "Aw shut up, Skeeter. You're laughin' at me"

"I'm not laughin' at you. I didn't think you cared what anybody thought. Nobody ever saw you in a dress."

"Daddy wanted me to wear a dress. What's the point of dressin' up, anyway? Why can't we just have fun the way we want to? Gene Vincent don't wear no proper white shirt and tie all the time. That's what rock 'n' roll's all about, ain't it? You told me that, Skeet. It's about kids havin' their own music and their own way of dancin' and about not bein' like grown ups. I ain't got no poodle skirt."

"Well, you look fine. I mean, OK. I mean, well …. Oh, don't worry about it"

"Yea? Well you look like a dope with slicked down hair and a silk noose around your neck. Plus, what's that, booger designs on your tie? Ah, ha, ha ha."

Skeeter laughed at that one, too. Whew. They seemed to be doing alright. Not for long, though, because climbing the steps was Linda Lewis, a rough neck. She had on too much lipstick, too much rouge, and high heels that looked like she borrowed them from Minnie Mouse.

Linda, the smart aleck pronounced. "Well, if isn't Jack and Jill havin' a night on the town?"

"Hi, Linda." Skeeter said without looking directly at her.

Jill not only looked directly at her, but stared holes right through her. Linda blew a Bazooka gum bubble at Jill's face. Jill blew a spit bubble in return.

"Sorry to break the news to you Jack," Linda said to Skeeter. "But if you think your Jill is Cinderella, you're in for a big surprise. Did you borrow that dress from you mother or your grandmother? Better get it back before midnight."

Oh no. This doesn't look good at all. Jill took a step toward Linda, the gum popper, to tell her to take it back. At the same micro millisecond, Linda's big brother, Lumpy, who the whole town knew had a bladder control problem, stepped in. Jill accidentally stepped on the tongue of one of Lumpy's big tennis shoes as he started to walk. Jill tripped and fell forward against Linda, pushing her to the concrete. Miss Bazooka got the breath knocked out of her, causing her gum to propel itself into Skeeter's hair. She landed flat on her butt. Jill braced herself against the wall and Lumpy veered off the entry and onto the grass.

"Hey, kid." Lumpy growled and headed for Jill. Jill headed for Lumpy. Executing her best football fake maneuver, Jill zipped by the big kid. Skeeter bolted toward Lumpy when he saw Lumpy's hand squeezing the hem of Jill's dress.

Skeeter dove at Lumpy's size 14 Converse All Stars. Lumpy hit the ground with the sound similar to that of a burlap bag full of mud falling off a cart.

All of this happened so fast, most of the cotillion go-ers never saw it. The few who did ran for the chaperones. They brought out Mrs. Ragsdale who was considerably old and quite nearsighted. "Is everyone having fun?" She smiled in the direction of the pile of little adults.

"Yes ma'am." They said in unison.

The rowdies got to their feet, brushed themselves off and pretended it never happened, all but Jill. Lumpy headed home to change.

Jill's face flushed. "Let's get outta' here."

"We can't leave yet. We have to tell our parents what a great time we had as adults." Skeeter made her think hard about this. "OK. Let's go back in the gym and pretend like everything's cool. We'll walk in separately. We'll talk to some of our friends. Then you and I'll dance together a couple of times."

"Dance?" Jill said. "I can't dance."

"You'll be OK. We'll get in the center of the floor and blend in with everybody else. Just do what I do."

"Like you can dance?"

Skeeter flashed a ridiculous smile. "You just watch, Jill-o."

"So, I'm supposed to look like I'm having a Gene at-tack too? What next?" Jill asked him.

"Tell everybody good-bye. Then tell Mrs. Price that you have to get home. I'll walk up and overhear you, then, I'll ask Mrs. Price if she thinks I should walk you home."

Jill spit at a bush. "Cool plan, buddy."

Skeeter's brain froze for about ten seconds. You know, Bud, like it feels when you gulp water and shaved ice.

She never called me 'buddy' before. Skeeter thought.

I must confess something to you now, Bud. A couple of weeks ago, Skeeter told me about a plan he concocted. When he was younger, he read a story about two boys becoming blood brothers. His fascination with it, a bond between best friends, has him convinced that he and Jill should make such a vow of loyalty. Skeeter knew now, more than ever, they should become blood brothers. He kept his small knife sharpened just for the right time and place to make it happen. He was prepared for the ceremony and after the struggles they survived together, tonight would be the night.

I am totally amazed with the horrific thought of it, poor little Jill being part of such. Oh, I know, Bud, she's tough and strong and all that, but it still hurts me to think about it.

How would they do it? I am perplexed. Would they cut each other? I feel ill already.

Who would be nobler?

"Go." Jill barked.

Through the glass panels in the school doors, I watched Jill walk toward the gym entrance. All of the glass there had thin silver wire inside it and my view was distorted. Anyway, Skeeter started some small talk with Mr. Carter, the chemistry teacher. He didn't understand why since he and chemistry were about as far apart as lemons and liver.

What does that mean? I mean, Skeeter wasn't exactly studious when it came to technical subjects. Well never mind that for now, I have this story to tell.

Some kid named Alice asked Jill. "You OK?"

"Yea, that jerk girl just really made me mad."

"She's nothin, anyway," Alice agreed.

Skeeter took calculated strides across the floor, determined not to bust into the Gene. He looked like his usual arrogant self. I really hate to say bad things about people, especially my young friend, but Skeeter is too big for his britches. Now, Bud, I'm not saying it will happen, but Skeeter needs his come-uppance.

Jill's dress was wrinkled, torn at one shoulder, and the hem had been pulled out in the front during her altercation. It was a necessary battle scar for a scrapper like Jill. She had managed to maintain her reputation while departing with some dignity. Their plan to leave worked.

"Was that awful or what?" Skeeter broke the silence while he pulled his necktie through his collar. He didn't realize that he had untied the perpetual knot in his tie. Since he didn't know how to tie a necktie, he'd have to get his father to tie it again the next time he had to wear the noose. "I told you it would be stupid." Skeeter said with his usual, 'I told you. I told you.' attitude.

"And, I told you it would be hilarious, Skeet, and it was. It wasn't stupid at all. It was funny as crap. All the Miss Prisses in their fancy dresses and all, pretending to be people they're not. And, did you see Wenus and Peanut and Shadrack all doing' some stupid stiff legged monster dance with each other? Ah, ha, ha, ha."

Skeeter prayed Jill hadn't seen him do the monster dance. He had actually invented it. You remain perfectly stiff except you swing your arms from the shoulder sockets and you walk stiff legged. Once Skeeter had given the monster dance instructions to them and got them going, he went for fruit punch.

"Where were you when the monster dance boys were going at it?" Jill asked him.

"Oh .... I must have been in a dark corner or with some girl practicing my own moves." Skeeter stopped walking to demonstrate.

"So, you danced with a girl?" Jill asked him. "I'm glad no boy asked me to dance."

"I danced with you once. What do you call that?"

"I call that, like, dancin' with my brother. Well, I've never danced with them either. Actually, dancin's purdy stupid anyway. I'd rather Indian wrestle somebody, anyway." Jill twisted her mouth to one side. Skeeter found this to be entertaining and liked watching her lips for some odd reason.

He stared at her. "Dancin' with your brother, huh?"

"Yea, my brother. You're my best friend, Llewellyn Whitmel, in the whole world. We know each other and who we are. We ain't pretentious. We are who we are and we fight to keep it that way. Except for your high and mighty ways, your arrogance, your need to make people think you're better than everyone else, and your attitude; well, you ain't bettern' anybody else. But, you're still my best friend." Jill had taken on the statue of a monster dancer.

"My arrogance, my high and mighty ways, my need to be better than everybody else, my attitude, and the rest, let's see. That's at least four things you have against me."

"Nah. There are more too." Jill stared him down.

"And you still like me?" Skeeter asked her.

"I didn't say I liked you. I said you're my best friend." They stood and looked at each other. "So. What do you think about that?" Jill demanded.

Skeeter turned away. "Come on. I only danced with you so somebody would."

"Yea? I only danced with you so you could say you danced with a girl and not with a bunch of other jerk boys doin' a monster dance. Not that you ever noticed or anything."

Skeeter walked toward King's Creek then started running. Of course Jill ran after him and in a short while she was running next to him.

CHAPTER 18

They slowed to a walk as Skeeter led the way to way to his boat. Jill heard, "untie her." It was Skeeter's usual command. She took the rope and broke the knot free.

Jill whispered. "We shouldn't be goin' out alone at night."

"The hell with it." Skeeter whispered back.

"Why are we whispering?" Jill asked her best friend.

"You started it. Anyway, it goes with the ceremony."

Jill wondered a few seconds then asked, "What ceremony?"

Skeeter didn't respond but kept busy getting the boat ready to shove off. He made sure the anchor line was secured to the bow and that it was coiled and free of knots. He felt really nervous plus he had drunk too much cotillion fruit punch. "Stay put. I'll be back in a minute."

Skeeter trotted across the soft sand far enough away that Jill couldn't hear what he was doing. When he was done he ran back as fast as he could.

Clouds filled the sky now, and there was barely enough light for them to see what they were doing. Any lights visible from town were too far away to interfere with their night vision.

"Get in." The boat's captain said.

Jill perched herself on the bow facing Skeeter. The temperature was just a few degrees cooler than being warm.

There were no sounds except those of the creek water licking the sides of the boat and the language the animals use when humans invade their night. A breeze from the west brought the delicious salt air from the Atlantic.

Jill thought it best she shouldn't ask about their destination. The hell with it. She repeated Skeeter's words to herself.

Silently, they drifted along the creek and into the hidden cove they called "the pocket." It was hidden from town, surrounded by tall pines. Skeeter rested the heavy oars in their places alongside the walls of the boat while it drifted on its course. Once the boat totally stopped forward motion, Skeeter gave the command to Jill. "Drop it over."

She lifted the galvanized anchor from beneath the bench and gently lowered it into the smooth dark water. The water parted under its weight and sucked it down the six feet beneath the boat until it rested in the soft silt below

What's this all about? Jill wondered. This is getting spooky. But Skeet's not tryin' to scare me. What's up with this?

The silence was interrupted by Skeeter's whisper. His voice was soft as silk. "You're not one bit scared are you Jilly?"

Jill shook her head. Skeeter could barely see her now. "I have never, on purpose, given you a reason to be afraid of me, have I?"

Her head gave the "no" signal again. "Best friends could never be afraid of each other." She breathed the words out as if a butterfly would have said them.

Then Skeeter told her. "This has to be done tonight, at this place, in this boat." Skeeter felt he should try to sound ceremonial and to convey a high degree of importance. "This is not a ritual. For neither of us will ever dare to reduce in any way the bonds of friendship and fidelity and honesty that we seal this night."

Skeeter surprised himself with his improvisation. He opened the water tight jar that held his emergency matches and candles. He motioned for Jill to sit Indian style with him in the bottom of the boat.

Jill didn't feel creepy, just the opposite was true. She felt an importance she had never felt outside her feelings for her family.

Skeeter slid the candle into its stand and handed the wax coated matches to his friend. Jill struck once, twice, and nothing but the smell of sulfur. On the third swipe across the rough edge of the box, the wooden splinter exploded with fire. The "pocket" appeared as they had never seen it before. Only for a second could they absorb their surroundings before the fire had reduced to no more than the tiniest flame.

Jill touched the fire to the wick and their eyes watched as the tiny candle took its place in the ceremony.

Skeeter began talking. "Jill, how we were sent to each other at the beginning of summer is a mystery to me."

"Me too." She said.

He went on. "We may think there are those against us. We feel no deep dislike for anyone."

"Except that jerk at the cotillion," Jill butted in. "Sorry."

"It's OK. I said no 'deep' dislike. You have shown me friendship that is without question and with total honesty. If you believe this to be true of me also, so answer." Skeeter said.

Jill tried not to giggle at that one. I must add that she's doing quite well.

"Skeeter, you have shown me friendship that is without question and with total honesty, too." Jill echoed.

Skeeter was on a roll now. Perhaps he had learned something in literature class. "As a spiritual bond can be created between two souls with signs and symbols, a physical bond, will, this night, seal forever our feeling of unconditional friendship, and loyalty."

Jill surprised herself with the tiny proclamation. "So be it."

Skeeter then produced a cardboard cigar box, adorned with bright colors, gold letters and Cuban words. "Excuse the box."

A physical bond? Jill thought. What could this be? She still wasn't afraid.

Skeeter took the small knife out of his pocket. From the box, he got a bottle of alcohol, and a new handkerchief, still in its plastic bag.

"I bought this at the gas station," he said. "Early in my life I learned the term 'blood brothers.' I have thought about this a lot and have planned to ask you about it for a long time. And for the way we stuck up for each other tonight, it has to be done now."

"I can't become a brother while wearing a dress. It's the first time you ever saw me in a stupid dress."

He assured her. "We'll consider it a disguise; a plot to confuse those who act against us."

"Well, I'm wearing boys' underwear anyway."

"Great," Skeeter said. He placed his thumb nail against the slot at the exposed edge of the blade and rotated it out of the handle until it snapped into place.

Jill blurted out, "As to our whereabouts after the cotillion and as to what has and will take place this night, shall be forever held in trust and secrecy deep within our two souls. Soon, there will be our one blood." Then she said to herself. "Man I'm good."

"This ceremony forever referred to as, 'The Night of the Pocket,' shall only be whispered between our four lips." Skeeter added.

I remained in silence above the shore, transfixed by these two. This, Bud, was far more than I ever anticipated.

Jill grabbed the sides of the boat as Skeeter leapt to his feet and shouted,

"Rueben, our black friend, in darkness we feel your presence and we welcome you as witness. We feel your guidance and welcome the light off your wings. Show yourself. Now!"

Skeeter's voice pierced the silence of 'the pocket' and made me shake until the branch upon which I stood vibrated and released tiny bits of dead bark.

"Come hither, crow." Jill shouted.

"Hither?" Skeeter said in Jill's direction.

"It sounded good didn't it?" She grinned.

I best do as requested if I'm to be immortalized in this story. A few healthy flaps and a slow glide later, my nails gripped the bow of the boat close to where Jill had been sitting.

"Prepare the dagger." Skeeter said to Jill.

"What dagger?" Jill asked Skeeter.

"The knife."

"Oh yea." Jill felt really stupid. She took the handkerchief and tore the bag open with her teeth. She unscrewed the top of the alcohol bottle and pressed the handkerchief over the top and tilted it until she felt the cool liquid on her fingertips. The acrid smell made them feel like this was somewhat of a medical procedure.

I had to turn away and stretch my beak out over the water to get a breath of fresh air. I couldn't be overcome from the vapors. Then who would finish the story?

Jill rubbed the cloth back and forth along each side of the blade; the sharp edge first, then the rest of the handle. She took the knife, cut the handkerchief in half, placed the cloth on the bench seat, and put the knife on top. Tilting the alcohol carefully, she wet the other half. "Hold out your hands."

Skeeter turned his palms upward and pushed them toward her. She held the back of his left hand and scrubbed his palm. Then she cleaned the right one. She placed this cloth on the seat and put the knife on it. Picking up the other cloth, she handed it and the bottle to Skeeter.

"Hold out your hands," he said. Skeeter held her hands first the left and then the right and washed them. "How do you want to do this?" He asked.

"In what way?"

"Do you want to cut me, or do you want me to cut myself?"

Jill answered. "Well. Do you want to cut yourself or do you want to cut me?"

Skeeter sat silently; thinking. "I don't want to hurt you," he said.

"I want you to cut me to prove to yourself that you can do it." Jill told him.

"Let's each cut ourselves, then, we'll cut each other. We'll cut each other's right hand after we cut our own left hands." He said.

"Very smart." Jill said.

"We'll mix our blood, left hand to left hand, because our left hands are closest to our hearts. Then right to right." Jill told him. Then she whispered, "I want to go first."

She picked up the knife and held out her left hand for Skeeter to see. She touched the blade to her skin near the center of her open hand. She stared into Skeeter's eyes and pressed the blade into her skin while pulling the knife with a slight slicing motion. Not hard enough. Again, she pressed and drew the knife, this time pressing down until she felt a sting. At the first hint of pain, she dropped the knife into the bottom of the boat. She moved her eyes from Skeeter to see what she'd done. Nothing. On the third try, they watched the crimson blood pool in her cupped hand.

"Here." Skeeter's voice interrupted the silence. He put out his hand for the knife.

I couldn't bear to look at Jill's hand. I felt as if I were going to faint.

"Rueben." Skeeter's voice made me look again. "Be witness to my best friend's pain."

I watched Jill pass the knife to Skeeter. Skeeter drew the knife across his palm, and like his friend, couldn't push hard enough to pierce his skin."

Come on, be a man, damn it. He urged himself on.

This time he barely stabbed the tip into his hand. But on the third attempt, he pressed harder and felt the blade slice into his palm. His blood now flowed like Jill's. Palms upward, they reached toward each other and, grasped each other's left hand, and pressed their palms together. Their bright red blood, now mixed together, dripped, indistinguishable, from their clasped hands, painting the gray floor of the boat.

They sat in silence and looked at each other until their mouths stretched into grins, then into teeth showing smiles.

"We did it." Jill said.

"Of course, we did." Skeeter answered.

I tried to gather my senses throughout the ordeal to keep from passing out. The friends squeezed their open wounds tightly together until the blood stopped flowing. Jill handed one of the handkerchief pieces to him and took the other for herself. They each wrapped the rags around their hands and made a fist.

"There is no need to hurt each buy cutting right hands. What we have done is evidence enough of truth, for and about each other." Skeeter proclaimed.

Then Jill thought up something to add.

"By our blood that now flows together, we cannot be separated or defined as two again. It is only one blood. Our hearts pump the same red blood. We stand as one."

I had a strange feeling come over me then. It was as though a squall would blow up without warning. Or, perhaps, it would hail. I had no time to think about it. The one thing, of which I was certain, was that these two needed to leave very fast. It was nearly ten o'clock and the cotillion ended at nine. They each needed to be home.

Skeeter reached for the alcohol bottle. He removed the rag from his hand and stared at his wound. He twisted open the metal lid. But, the blood in his palm was still slippery wet and the bottle slid from his fingers.

Jill saw it falling and reached for it. So did Skeeter. The bottle hit the bottom of the boat. Air rushed in and forced the liquid to burp out and onto the floor where they sat. Both Jill and Skeeter jumped up at the same time to keep the alcohol off their clothes. The boat rocked hard. And, as if in slow motion, the lighted candle tumbled over and appeared to gently float through space and into the flammable liquid.

With a huge "whoosh," the alcohol ignited with the intensity of a small bomb. "The pocket" erupted with light. The smell of the burning liquid brought, fear to our hearts. Hundreds of creatures gasped with fright, too, as the light temporarily blinded them. Birds took flight toward the safety of the open sky. The force of their wings stirred up the air like the sound of a summer hurricane.

Skeeter looked horrified. Jill was nearly frozen with fright.

CAW! CAW! CAW! CACK! CACK! CACK! I wished I could scream out that the hem of Jill's dress was on fire and burning up her back. Then Skeeter saw it too.

"Jump! Jump! Get in the water!" Skeeter reached out to push her over the side.

I could see Jill was so scared she couldn't think. She saw the horror in Skeeter's eyes as his hands flew at her. Without thinking, Jill leaned toward the water and let herself fall. Skeeter dove in from the other side.

My heart nearly stopped as they splashed into the dark night water. I jumped off too, circled the boat, and headed for shore. I landed on the sand, raised my wings high as I could, and watched for their heads to pop up on each side of the boat.

Jill felt the bottom with her shoe and realized the water wasn't very deep. She was able to stand with her head out of the water. Skeeter stood up right away.

They each cupped their hands and managed to throw enough water in the boat to put the flames out.

"You OK?" Jill gasped.

"Yea." Skeeter coughed. "My hand hurts, but, I'm OK. Look at that mess."

I flapped my wings upward and lit on the bow.

"You OK, Rue?" Jill turned her head to me.

I replied by taking a few steps toward her and jerking my head. What a relief they weren't hurt. The fire was now out.

"I wonder what time it is. Our parents are gonna' kill us if they can't find us." Skeeter said.

"I think we're OK. Even if the other kids are heading home they'll know we're together." Jill told him.

I watched them bail the black water out of the boat. The alcohol that didn't burn had now evaporated. Actually, there was so little alcohol left, the floor of the boat was only slightly blackened. It would be bleached out by the sun in a month or so.

They guided the boat to the beach so they could easily climb back in. I knew Jill's dress was ruined. Not that she'd have occasion to wear it soon. The sleeves were ripped too.

"I'm freezin.'" Jill was shaking.

"Well. I'm sorry. I'm cold too. What do you want me to do about it? I'll row as fast as I can."

Jill was tough as any boy. "It's OK. I'll be alright."

Skeeter realized what he said. "Why did I act ugly to her? You idiot."

"Look. I'm sorry I just yelled at you. I don't know why I did it."

"It's OK." Jill wasn't going to let him ruin her night by continuing the conversation.

I flew ahead and soon we were out of "the pocket" and across King's Creek. With just the moonlight, I watched them tie the boat to the dock.

The reflection of the knife blade under the bench caught Jill's eye. She picked it up and folded the blade back into the handle. "Here."

Skeeter took it from her and dropped it into his pants pocket. "Thanks."

"What are we gonna' say we were doin'?" Jill asked him.

"Well. We'll just say everything happened as it did. Except for the ceremony, it was an accident."

CHAPTER 19

During the next several days, Skeeter was occupied with grass mowing jobs and any other chores he could do to earn money for the Gene show. I flew along with him and scratched around his customers' shrubs looking for anything interesting. One boring day, for Skeeter, was spent traveling up the shore with his mother and visiting several of their relatives. Skeeter managed to hide his knife wound from his parents for the first few days. But, as they got in the car to leave home, his mother noticed him rubbing his palm.

"What's wrong with your hand, Honey?"

"Oh, nothin', it just itches."

"Are you sure it's ok? You've been rubbing it a lot the last day or so."

"I'm fine, honest." Skeeter assured his mother.

I watched him settle into the shotgun position of the family car as his mother crept along Monroe then right on Fig. I flew along with them for a few blocks. Skeeter had a silly grin on his face that turned into a smile that only he and I could understand. I knew he was reliving the blood brothers ceremony over and over in his mind. I was sure of it because I still had a bad feeling about it.

It was on Friday morning that Skeeter headed out to Jill's house. Although he had been busy with his chores, he missed being with her and the fun they had together. They had seen each other almost every day since they'd met.

Chapter 19

When we got to Peach Street and saw her house, the oddest feeling came over both of us. Something in the air was terribly wrong. I could see it on Skeeter's face. It was very strange, indeed.

Skeeter hopped up on her, porch knocked on the door, and waited. He thought about school starting soon, but blocked it out of his mind. The living room appeared the same as he had seen before, but he'd never been inside.

He knocked again and called. "Jill? Jilly, are you here? Is anybody home?"

There was no answer, only silence. He went to the door leading from outside to the dining room. He then went to the kitchen door. On the kitchen table he saw plates with food left on them. He called out again and again, still no answer. Skeeter liked poking around vacant buildings, but this was too much. His blank gaze led me to believe his mind was spinning with thoughts of his friend and her family being missing. He turned the door knob of the back door. It was cold and clammy. It turned freely and the latch released. Not letting go of the knob, he pushed the door open and called out again. An unfinished meal and sour milk, clinging to the inside of their glasses, was most troubling to the both of us. It looked like they had left in a hurry.

Skeeter stepped back from the door, closed it, and made sure it was latched like we found it. I flew around to the front of the house and returned to the porch roof where I had danced for Jill on cotillion night. I could see no clue to where she may be.

Skeeter walked across Peach Street and looked up at Jill's bedroom windows but saw nothing unusual. Clouds crossed in front of the sun and the sky was turning gray. A cool breeze stirred off the bay. What started out as a perfect summer day was now turning dreary. "Let's go Rue. She can't be too far away."

I flew high above Skeeter as he rode his bike toward the beach and the Pavilion. Not there. South to Randolph, we looked around the Northampton Hotel grounds. Skeeter got off his bike and pushed it passed the store fronts and peered in the windows.

"How's the arm, Skeeter?"

"It's ok." Skeeter answered a man carrying a sack of potatoes. "Have you seen that new girl lately?"

"You mean the tomboy?"

"Yes Sir."

"I saw her and one of them gypsy kids last week. Ain't seen her lately though. She probably ain't far."

"Ok. Thanks."

Another man said. "Hey there, Skeeter. Hey Rueben, have a peanut." The man tossed some nuts on the sidewalk out of the way of people walking by. Again, Skeeter asked about Jill. I picked up a nut and crushed it with a single bite. I ate the goober and flew ahead of Skeeter and listened. No one had seen her lately.

Skeeter got back on his bike and took off to the school. Willie T hadn't seen her since the cotillion. There was no sign of her on the ball field. The trip to Kings Creek turned up no clues either. The boat sat scorched, just as we'd left it.

"This is all my fault." Skeeter said to me. "Why do I think I have to be so cool all of the time? I shouldn't have made her cut herself." I gripped the front rail of the boat and cocked my head back and forth listening. The sky was darker now and the wind was chilly. I left the front rail of the boat and hopped on Skeeter's shoulder and we stared at the boat together.

"Standin' here ain't helping us find her," he said. Back on the bike, Skeeter rode back to town. "Maybe I should go back to the gypsy camp." Skeeter told me. "After all, the kid did sort of invite me." Skeeter also had nothing better to do. He made sure he had his knife in this pocket though. His bike danced across the hard rough road and right onto Fig Street. In the middle of the street he built up speed, took his feet off the pedals and coasted for a block. Legs straight out to each side, he felt like he was flying low.

"Caw, Caw." Up above him about as high as the roof of his house, I caught up with him. Skeeter headed east out of town, past the railroad shops toward the gypsies. This time he didn't have to hide his curiosity as he had done before. He would bike right in because he was invited, sort of. Most important, maybe he could find Jill.

He peddled up close to where the boy had startled him. This time as he saw the cars he slowed down and got off his bike. He walked it up close to the first vehicle, put down the kick stand and stood for a few minutes. There was no music this time and no dancing. Skeeter moved in closer and called out. "Hello?" He saw some shadows and movement behind a tent. "Hello? Anybody here?" He called.

"Who is here?" A woman's voice, deep and bossy, bounced off the metal of the vehicles. It wasn't a welcoming tone of voice like Skeeter's mom had.

"Yikes." Skeeter said. "My name's Skeeter and I am looking for a boy my age." He heard his own words come out before he had a chance to plan what he was saying. "I was here last week."

Skeeter watched the tent and saw a lady walk toward him. She didn't smile but she didn't frown either. Her white blouse had ruffles all over and it made her dark skin look beautiful. She had colored makeup on her eyelids and around her eyes. Deep red lipstick and her big hoop earrings made Skeeter think that she must be a movie star.

"Why do you want to see a boy your age?" She stared at Skeeter.

Well.....well, he thought. Why did he want to see a boy his age? "He asked me to come back." Skeeter stammered.

"He did? Yes?" The painted lady questioned. "And you want to see my son again also too?"

"If you don't mind, ma'am."

"Come." Skeeter followed as she turned and headed back toward the tent. She stopped and spun around to Skeeter and just slightly smiled. "It will be good for him to see you. He has been working very hard."

Up in the sky a small black blur glided into Skeeter's view. Of course, it was me. Looking past the lady, Skeeter saw me light in a tall pine far away. I kept my distance from the camp.

That's odd. Skeeter thought to himself. Rueben always likes to be around me.

As they continued walking, I flew a little closer. The lady shrieked when she saw the black streak. "If I had my gun I would shoot and kill that black devil bird. They bring us bad luck. Bad, bad luck." She held her arms up as if she were holding a gun with both hands. With her head cocked to one side and with one painted eye closed, "Pow!" she yelled.

At the exact same time as her pretend shotgun went off, we heard the familiar sound of a real shotgun. There across the field stood a gypsy man holding a shotgun to his shoulder. Skeeter watched a small trail of smoke rise from the barrel.

Skeeter no longer saw me. I wasn't in the sky and he didn't see me perched in any tree. Skeeter had grown up with hunters and hunting. He had shot his share of game and had eaten what he killed. How could anyone want to hurt Rueben? He thought. He doesn't hurt anybody.

"No, Father. No, Father." The gypsy boy ran toward the man with his arms and hands waving. He came running from a group of cars along the same path his mother was leading Skeeter. Skeeter started to run too. He ran after the boy and caught up with him as he got to his father. The man rested the stock of the gun on the ground and leaned it against his hip. A big hairy grin came on the man's face, teeth barely visible behind a big black moustache.

"Hold on there boy." the man said in his thick accent. "I was only once to try to frighten the bad luck out of that black menace. A rook that black and big will be no good to live here. But, killing the bird would have bring to us worse luck."

"Oh," the boy said. He looked up at his father with respect, believing what he had heard.

Skeeter didn't believe the man. He thought the man would kill me if the boy hadn't been there. I thought so, too.

"Who is this intruder? Do you come to run us off of your land?

"No Sir." Skeeter said politely.

"Well what then? Tell me."

"I asked him to come and play, Father." The boy jumped in. He thought Skeeter might be afraid of his father's loud voice and broken English.

"Who has time for play in the middle of the day? Men have work to be done."

"I finished my project." The boy said.

"You are right boy. I forgot." The moustache stopped moving for a minute. "Go on then and have some fun. I will check your work when you return."

"Thank you Father."

"Thank you Sir." Skeeter added.

"Let's go then. Come on." Gypsy boy shouted.

The two boys ran through a field of grass and chased each other across the soft farm land. "Follow me." Skeeter yelled. Their figures were soon swallowed up by the old oak grove that divided two farms. When they were out of breath, the two slowed to a walk and then just stopped.

"Your father scared me good." Skeeter finally said.

"How so?" The boy asked.

"I thought for sure he was going to kill Rueben!"

"Who is Rueben?"

"Next to ...." Skeeter hesitated. "He's my best friend. Rueben is a crow."

"How can a crow be your best friend?"

"I have a lot of friends from town. Rueben's a friend I can tell stuff to that I can't tell anybody else. Plus, he can keep a secret."

"Ha. Ha." The boy laughed. "Then you are lucky to have such a friend."

"My name is Django. I am glad that you came back. My family moves from place to place and we must be careful who we talk to. I think that you are a good junior man."

"A junior man? What is a junior man?" Skeeter asked.

"A junior man learns from his father and his uncles how to work with his hands and to make things. A junior man also studies his religion and family customs. Once he can make things to sell or when he learns to repair other people's things for money, he is one step closer to becoming a man. Another part is knowing and practicing the customs and the traditions and the religion of his people. Once he learns these things and knows the past of his ancestors, he may become a man."

"Wow," Skeeter thought. He couldn't think of anything to say. He didn't think that he was even a junior man. Skeeter felt pretty stupid. He never really thought about much other than being a kid and, of course, getting to see Gene.

"What kind of name is Django?"

"What kind of name is Skeeter?" The boy shot the same question back to Skeeter.

"Skeeter's just a nick name."

"Why are you ashamed of your name that you have to use a false name? One that is untrue?"

"I'm not ashamed of my name. Skeeter is what I have been called since I was a baby. My cousin, was killed in World War II. His nick name was Skeeter, so everyone just started calling me that in his honor. I'm proud that I am named after my cousin."

"I see. You are lucky two times, one for Rueben and one for Skeeter."

"What about you?" Skeeter looked at his new friend. "Are you really a Gypsy?"

"Gypsies are what people call us. But, we are really Roma or Rom." He said.

"Roma? Like for roaming around?"

Django laughed at what Skeeter had said and thought he had tried to make a joke.

"No, not like that," Django explained. "My family comes from many places around the world. But, the first people, you call Gypsies, came from the north of India."

Skeeter heard Django's words but wasn't listening. He remembered the reason he had come. It was to look for Jill.

"I gotta' find Rueben. Help me find him, Django. I gotta' find Jill."

No one saw me flying away from the camp after the shotgun blast. I kept low to the ground and flew as fast as possible. I turned my head to see if Django's father was going to shoot at me again. When I saw the shotgun resting on the ground, I quit flapping and sailed along in relief. But, the second time I looked back, I sailed beak first into a stand of cattails and slid to the ground. It was here that Skeeter and Django found me.

"Rue," I heard Skeeter call. "Are you alright? Can you stand up?"

Skeeter tucked my wings to my sides and rubbed my head. Slowly I began to catch my breath. The boys sat on the ground next to me. I was very dizzy.

"Stand up, boy. Can you stand up?"

I wasn't at all comfortable being so close to Django. After all, his father called me names and tried to kill me.

"Cack," I said to Skeeter. "Cack, Cack." I yelled in Django's direction.

Slowly I pushed myself up until I felt my feet on the ground beneath me. I wobbled away from them and flapped myself off the ground and into the air.

"Looks like he's OK," Django said.

"Yea. He's a tough old bird."

"Look. The reason I came out here is to see if you have seen a friend of mine who is missing."

"What does he look like?"

"Well, he's actually a girl but kinda dresses like a boy. A man in town told me that he thought saw her talking to a gypsy kid a few days ago. Have you seen her?"

"No, my friend, I do not know her."

CHAPTER 20

Skeeter had never actually been in Jill's house before, except for one step inside the kitchen this morning. Still no one answered the banging of his fists on the door. Now, we had to go in. Something inside me knew I needed to help Skeeter find our friend.

He crept into the dining room from the kitchen, then into the parlor. There was still no sign of anyone being there. With me on his shoulder, we climbed the stairs to the landing, stopped, and Skeeter called out again. Jill had told him that her bedroom was on the front of the house and he had seen her wave to him through her window. He peered into each of the rooms as he passed the doorways. There were no blankets or sheets on the beds. Skeeter had never felt before what he was feeling. Was he scared? He didn't think so. Was he going to be sick? He wasn't sure.

He wanted to see her room, but he didn't want to know for certain that she was gone. He hoped so much that she would be standing behind her door waiting to jump out and yell at him for being in her house.

After what seemed like hours, we got to her door. From the hall he could see across the room and out through the window. He moved his head from right to left studying the bare floor. Her bed was stripped, too. No bed clothes. Her closet door was open. No clothes in there. The dresser drawers were left open as if someone in a hurry had emptied them, not caring about leaving them neatly closed.

Skeeter had never felt so confused. Where could her family be and why did they leave in such a hurry? He wondered. Would he ever see her again? He wished she'd sneak up behind him, yell "April fools" and knock him to the floor.

Skeeter needed to tell someone what we had seen. He spun around fast toward the door and bolted toward it. Out of the corner of his eye something caught his attention. He pushed the door almost closed and bent down to the floor. There was a small red leather book leaning against the baseboard where the door was hinged to the wall. Skeeter picked it up, stood silently, and studied it. There was a strap sewn on the one side that had a brass hook on it. On the cover side was a brass lock sewn into the cover. The strap wasn't locked into place.

Oh no, he thought. I hope it's not her diary. Printed across the closed edges on the bottom side he saw, J I L L, drawn with black ink.

He held it with both hands and squeezed the book shut. He started to slip the hook into the lock but stopped. What if it won't open again? I'd better not. He shifted the diary to his left hand, pulled the door open and headed to the hall. He went down the stairs, then out the back door where we'd come in. Skeeter couldn't stand still. He ran to the rear of the back yard to look at the back of the house. Where could they be? He kept thinking.

Something in the yard of the house next door waved at him. It was the neighbor's wash, hanging out to dry. The bay breeze lifted the damp clothes up and down from the clothes line. Row, after row, of white unmentionables, upside down at times, danced around like clouds. Between the clothes lines was Jill's neighbor, Mrs. Kerr, hanging up more.

"Mrs. Kerr, Mrs. Kerr," Skeeter shouted, as he trotted toward her. "What happened to this family? Do you know where they are?" Skeeter was starting to loose his breath.

"Slow down there Skeeter," she said. "First, I don't have a clue as to where they are or might be. Second, it's none of my business, or yours, as I see it. I'm not some old gossip lady telling things I really don't know about."

Skeeter told her. "I'm not being nosey, well, for once anyway, but I hope they're not hurt or in trouble."

The neighbor smiled and chuckled a little. "I do know this. I'm sure they're not gone for good. So don't go getting yourself all sweaty about that part of it."

"That part of it? That part of what, ma'am?" Skeeter couldn't hear the story fast enough.

"Now I'm no busy body and you didn't hear this from me because I keep to myself." Her eyes shot to the diary. "What's that? She growled."

"Huh? What?" Skeeter grunted.

"In your hand," she pointed.

"Oh", Skeeter stared down at Jill's sacred book. "Ah, it's just a book of mine."

"What's that painted on the edge? What's it say?"

Skeeter looked hard at Jill's unmistakable name. He held the book so that her name was upside down. "It just says 771 and, and,"

"And, what?"

"And I made a mistake trying to print the 5." Skeeter was thinking fast. He was sorry that he had to tell a lie.

The woman stared at the book then looked at Skeeter. "Anyway," she said, "two days ago the Sheriff's deputy went up on the porch and knocked on the door. I wasn't bein' nosey but I was sweepin' my front steps when he came up."

"What happened then?"

She paused for a long time. "You run along now," she said. "You're too young to be hearing such. Go on, git! And, you better stay away from that house."

Skeeter remembered his father was taking the day off from work and would probably be home. He rode the half block of Peach Street then he cut across the park grounds to Monroe. I thought we'd never get home. He held the diary as tightly as he could. Passing the front door, he slowed down to turn right to pass the side door of his house too.

"Dad! Dad!" Good, he was about done cutting the grass.

His dad stopped pushing the grass cutter when he saw Skeeter coming toward him.

"What's all the excitement about, son?"

Skeeter couldn't talk. He was too out of breath. He stood with his hands on his knees, half bent over. His face was bright red. He tried to tell what he just learned, but no words came out. It seemed like an hour went by before he heard sounds stammering out his mouth.

"My friend Jill and her family are gone. They just disappeared. All of their stuff is gone from their house, too. Their dinner was left half eaten on their dishes. Where could she…, I mean, where could they be? The neighbor lady started to tell me about the Sheriff's deputy knocking on their door, but then she stopped and ran me off."

News travels fast in every small town, and Cape Charles was no different. Skeeter's father had heard something a few days ago, but didn't think any more about it.

"Well, it seems that the father got hurt a year or two ago and couldn't work. Because he couldn't work, there wasn't any money to pay for a place to live and for food and electricity and for anything else."

"But, he has a job now." Skeeter was confused.

"Yes, I think he does. But, I heard that he owed some people money and now they want it back." Skeeter's dad tried to explain this to Skeeter as best he could.

"But, why did he leave and take his family? Where did they go?"

"I just don't know, Son. Maybe he thought runnin' away would give him time to figure out a plan."

Skeeter rubbed his hand across his forehead. "It doesn't seem fair."

Chapter 20

"I know, Son. Maybe we'll hear some good news about them soon."

Skeeter backed toward the street a few steps. He pushed hard on the scar on his hand hoping it would stop throbbing.

His father heard him mumble, "Thanks for tellin' me."

CHAPTER 21

Skeeter felt a sick helplessness. He wished he could help Jill's family somehow. He was still holding the diary and didn't realize it. His father didn't ask about it either. Maybe he didn't notice it, unlike the busybody neighbor. Skeeter looked at his hand and saw his white knuckles squeezing the book as if the words may escape. Now, the scar started itching again.

"Her diary." Skeeter said quietly.

He looked around to see if anyone was watching him, and was relieved to see no one. This diary had to be kept a secret. Skeeter dashed behind a big shrub. He lifted up the bottom of his shirt and slipped the secret book half way down the back of his pants, held in place by his belt. He pulled his shirt back down over it and felt to see if any-one would know he was now a book smuggler. He stepped from behind the shrub and walked as if nothing unusual were going on. Through the dining room to the kitchen he crept. He was on the lookout for his mom. The path was clear. He silently slid up the stairs and down the hall to his room. Once there, he closed the door so as not to be discovered. Then he opened it with the same swift move. A closed door would be suspicious. Good thinking.

Skeeter moved across his room to a corner where there was enough light to read. He pulled the red book from his pants, got down on the floor, and leaned against the wall. Holding the book against his knees, he focused on the front cover. He stared at it without really thinking about it. He turned it to one side and stared at the straight lines that spelled Jill's name. Pushing it into his pants had caused it to latch.

Skeeter stretched his finger toward the round brass button that would release the diary's lock. His finger rested on it a second. Don't do that. He thought. That's her personal stuff. She'd kill me if I opened it. She'd kill me worse if I actually read anything in it. Skeeter's hand flew off the latch like it was a hot skillet.

Jill couldn't stand anyone touching her stuff anyway. Even though she didn't have many things that were totally hers, she hated it if someone borrowed something and didn't put it back exactly where it was.

Skeeter wondered why he would read it anyway. What was the answer to this? Perhaps there were clues to where she and her family had gone. Or maybe, she described being kidnapped. Maybe she would want Skeeter to know what was on the last few pages. Skeeter thought about giving it to the Sheriff for him to read for clues. He was totally confused.

I studied Skeeter as he struggled.

No, he would not betray a friend. He had to keep this a huge secret.

For some strange reason, Skeeter wondered if I had seen the diary in his hands. Ha, ha, hah. Of course I'd seen it. I saw him take it in the first place. I actually had some difficulty shoving it across Jill's bedroom floor near the door where he found it. I had to make sure he'd see it when he was poking around in her house.

"Rue. We have to keep this to ourselves. Don't let on that we have it until the time is right."

I watched and listened to Skeeter and cocked my head to signal that he could, of course, trust me.

It was terribly uncomfortable for me knowing that Skeeter was so upset. I wasn't sure, either, about where she was. But, I'm sure I saw her father's car speeding out of town four nights ago. I had no idea Jill might be involved. I couldn't help myself any longer. Skeeter had to know what was happening or he'd burst. I walked around nervously while Skeeter stared at the book. I had an idea. I walked to the edge of the book and started pecking at the latch.

"Stop." Skeeter whispered.

I jerked my head up and down and walked in an awkward circle.

Skeeter frowned at me. "Don't mess with it."

I had to get Skeeter to open that latch. Next, I stretched my foot out to try to push on the latch.

"What are you doing? Black bird. Crow. You black wizard. Black wizard? Where did I hear that? Who said that to me, Rue?" Skeeter fell back on his bed and searched his ceiling for the answer. "I know." Skeeter sat up. The fortune teller yelled 'black wizard' at you. You are the black wizard aren't you Rue?"

I was unsure how to act. I stepped up to the book and pecked my beak on the diary's lock. Tap, tap, tap, three times. Then, three times again. Skeeter should catch on soon. I was yelling to myself in crow language. Tap, Tap, Tap. Open this book. I wanted to scream.

Skeeter reached out for the book at last. I backed away from the latch hoping he would understand that's what I wanted him to do.

"Are you tellin' me to read this, Rueben, you black wizard?" Skeeter pressed his thumb into his scar and tried to make the throbbing go away.

I walked in a circle now, twisting my head and trying to make my sharp toe nails loud as possible. I stopped and tapped at the book three more times. Finally, Skeeter lifted the book and turned it to the bottom edge and stared at the angular letters, J I L L, that his friend had printed. Skeeter pushed the latch and the clasp came undone. It wasn't locked as he had feared. The flap opened and his eyes were inside. Wow, Skeeter thought. She sure writes a lot. I only wrote in mine three times.

He thought once again about betraying her. He was determined not to. He would only read the last few entries to see if there would be a clue to where she was. He fingered his way to the last page with writing on it.

TUESDAY

August 21, 1956

Dear diary,

I don't feel any better today. My rash is redder and I know Daddy will see it soon. I'm so cold even under my blanket. I took my temperature and it was 101 F a little while ago. I have to go fix dinner now. Daddy and my brothers will be home soon. I'm fryin' chicken for them. I threw up three times so far.

MONDAY

August 20, 1956

Dear diary,

I feel worse today. I have the sweats. But, I'm cold at the same time. I can't help crying and I hate it. My hand looks real bad. It is bright red near the cut and it's turning purple near my fingers. Daddy will kill me if he finds out we cut ourselves on purpose. Skeeter hasn't come to my house. I need to tell him. He'll know what to do.

Later. I took some aspirin, but, I don't feel better. Skeeter will get in trouble too. His mother will get mad because he made a girl cut herself on purpose. But, he didn't make me. I don't think they'll believe me.

Later. I'm in bed now. I'm sweating like mad but freezing cold inside. Rueben is on the porch roof just outside my window. I like to talk to him and tell him secrets. He keeps me company. I wish I could stop crying like a sissy.

I'll pray that I'm better in the morning. I wish Skeeter would come over.

Skeeter and I both felt sick as he read the entries to me.

"Rueben, where was I? Why didn't I go to her house?" Skeeter kept reading.

SUNDAY
August 19, 1956
Dear Diary,
Last night was the best night ever. My plan to some day do something noble and brave finally came true. I'll write about the cotillion later. The best part is that me and Skeeter left the cotillion early because of the fights. Oh, forget that for now. Anyway, my hand hurts real bad. That's because Skeeter and I became blood brothers last night. It happened in Skeeter's boat. I have to go now.
Sunday night now. I threw up three times today. My hand hurts really bad. I can't tell Daddy. He'll think that was stupid and we'll be in real trouble, the kind of trouble that makes you sick in your stomach. More later. I hope I can get warm soon.

SATURDAY
August 18, 1956
Dear Diary,
Tonight is the cotillion night. It is going to be great fun. I wish I did not have to wear a stupid dress. But, it will

be fun seeing the other kids wearing coats and real neck ties. I cannot wait to watch the dancing. What if a boy asks me to dance? I don't know how. I will politely refuse. Or if it's one of my friends, I'll just cuss him out. Well, no boy will ask me anyway. I know for sure, Skeeter, Wenus, and Shadrack won't dance. Maybe some teenagers will boy-girl dance. More later.

Saturday night. I must write something, but I'm too tired now. My hand hurts a little. It was the best night ever. More in the morning.

Skeeter reread Tuesday's entry.

CHAPTER 22

"She's real sick, isn't she Rueben? Is she in a hospital? She didn't tell her father she was sick so we wouldn't get in trouble. So I wouldn't get in trouble."

Skeeter was sick inside. He opened his hand and said, "Why did I do that? What a stupid fool. I gotta' tell."

Skeeter tapped his shoulder and I hopped on. I hoped he wouldn't run down the stairs with me. That always makes me sick.

Skeeter's mother sprinkled water on a wrinkled dress that was piled up on her ironing board. When the hot iron was pushed across the fabric it gave off thick steam that made the house smell warm and comfortable.

Skeeter's mom had to calm him down several times, so she could put all the pieces together. The cotillion, something about blood brothers, a diary....

"Slow down son. My, my, help me sort this out."

Skeeter finally got the story in order. He wasn't thinking about being in trouble anymore.

"Bless her heart." Skeeter's mother had a lady's white hanky and was wringing it in her hands. She was thinking real hard. After staring at the floor a bit, she went into the hallway and sat in a chair that had a table attached to it. It was a regular piece of furniture built to hold a person and a telephone. It had a shelf beneath it where the telephone directory was kept. By memory, she dialed the town doctor's phone.

Chapter 22

"Flora. This is Mrs. Whitmel. We need some help here. What? Lord have mercy, no. Everything's just fine. The little girl, Jill, who lives with her father on Peach Street, do you know anything about her? That's right, the tomboy. Yes, she does look like a boy occasionally. Well, she and her family seem to have gone missin' and Skeeter thinks she may have blood poisoning and may have been taken to a hospital. I can't go into detail now. OK. OK. Thanks. I'll be waitin' to hear from you."

"What Mom? What?"

"Well, that was Flora who works for…"

"I know. Dr. Griffith." Skeeter snapped.

"Don't pitch a hissie fit, son."

"Sorry, what did she say?"

"Well, the good doctor is going to visit patients in DePaul hospital in Norfolk tomorrow. She is goin' to ask him to try to find out something about her."

"Why did you tell her Jill has blood poisoning?"

"Well honey the symptoms you told me about point that way."

"Jeez, that sounds real bad. Thanks, Mom. Let's go Rue."

We were miserable. We couldn't do anything knowing Jill was sick. Or worse. No! I will not think about it being worse. Poor Skeeter. This is such troubling news for a boy who wanted to spend his summer having as much fun as possible.

I stayed on Skeeter's shoulder much of the day. We took the diary back up to Skeeter's room. He read each entry out loud. He read only what she'd written since the day of the cotillion, nothing before that. Skeeter still believed that was private.

"This is my fault, Rueben. It was my idea to become blood brothers. I sharpened the knife. I prepared all of the tools. I set the stage for her to get blood poisoning. I'm selfish and I'm arrogant, too."

I walked up Skeeter's arm and onto his shoulder again. Then, Bud, I got a wonderful idea. I hopped onto the window sill and pecked at the screen. I jerked my head a bit and got Skeeter's attention.

"You want out, boy?"

I pecked again. Skeeter unlatched the screen and pushed it open far enough for me to get out. I flapped only twice and glided down, homing in on Skeeter's bike. I nearly slipped off the chrome handlebars. I managed to bite the wire of the basket and caught my balance. I turned back to face the house and looked in Skeeter's direction.

It wasn't long before I heard Skeeter's thump, thump, thump, on the stairs. When I was sure he was coming outside, I took flight. I flew circles around his bike hoping he'd get the message. When he grabbed the handle grips, I flew west toward the beach.

Skeeter peddled behind. I didn't want to rush. I was trying to kill some time. We had a long wait before we would get word from Dr. Griffith. We went left along Nectarine then right on Randolph; each kept silent. There was no shouting or whooping it up. I could see the steeple long before Skeeter.

179

Chapter 22

Once at St. Charles Catholic Church, I knew better than to get too close to the building itself. I may have been swatted at or even smacked with a broom. I lit on the ground nearby and joined several brother crows who were scavenging near the concrete sidewalk. For a moment, Skeeter seemed puzzled, but only for a moment. He leaned his bike against a crepe myrtle tree. I watched as he pushed his thumb down on the brass latch and leaned against the dark oak door. Would I ever know what went on inside? I couldn't see through the stained glass and I dare not try to enter. I am a very curious bird, but I stayed outside.

I wasn't interested in sticking my beak into the earth like my buddies. I couldn't do anything but think about Jill's health and Skeeter's worry. After a seemingly endless wait, the huge door creaked open again. Skeeter appeared. He was not alone.

"Skeeter, please forgive me for interrupting your prayers. I didn't know you were here. I am glad that we had the chance to talk." It was Father Ryan, the priest.

Skeeter tried to act holy. "It's OK, Father. I feel a little better now."

"Tell your parents I said hello. I'll be praying for Jill and her family."

Skeeter walked toward his bike and squeezed the grips. "Thank you."

Skeeter got on his bike and rode to Kings Creek. He walked around his boat making sure all the lines were secured. I watched him do the oddest thing. He took a handful of beach sand and dropped it in the bottom of the boat. I watched from the bow as he searched for something along the beach. He picked up a piece of driftwood that was gray and smooth on the top and sides. Then, he brushed off some bugs that were hiding on the damp side of it. He knelt in the bottom of the boat and started scrubbing. He used the driftwood to rub the sand back and forth across the dark stain the fire had made.

"I don't ever want to see these char marks again, Rueben."

He scrubbed and scraped the bottom until he couldn't see any evidence of the fire. Skeeter untied the boat and hauled it out of the water onto the sandy beach. He walked to his bike and felt around in the basket. He took out a can of dark blue paint, a brush, and some paint thinner to clean his brush. He studied a sheet of paper and drew marks on it with a pencil. I couldn't make out what he was doing. It looked as if he were practicing drawing or something. When he stopped, he took the paint supplies to the stern of the boat and made himself a comfortable seat in the sand. Skeeter worked until it was almost dark.

"Let's go, boy. I hope I'm tired enough to be able to sleep all night."

I perched outside the Whitmel's house until I saw Skeeter's light go out. I found a safe place in a nearby elm tree and tried to sleep too. I managed to dose off with one eye open.

CHAPTER 23

After breakfast the next morning, Skeeter's mother handed out job after job.

As soon as he'd finish one, she'd get him to do something else. Skeeter didn't realize it, but she was simply trying to keep his mind occupied. Fretting can be a lonely burden. The telephone rang on several occasions. Each time it was someone who wanted to yak it up with Skeeter's mom. Skeeter stood in front of her and motioned his arms frantically for her to hang up. The nurse, Flora, might be trying to call.

It was nearly five o'clock that evening. It had been the longest summer day in history. Skeeter was kicking a football round Monroe Avenue when we heard his mother call. "Let's go Rue. Maybe Mom's heard some news."

Skeeter, with me clinging tight to his shoulder, ran toward his mother's voice. I spread my wings out as far as possible to keep my balance, but I couldn't.

Whoosh. Whoosh. I left Skeeter and flew ahead to the house. I circled the back yard, waited for Skeeter to catch up and then pass me. The screen door slammed behind him.

Bud. You just can't imagine what its like to be flying at twenty miles per hour and have a screened door slammed in your beak. I couldn't stop and I had no room to turn. There was nothing I could do to stop.

"Oh, no." I heard Skeeter call out.

I blinked my eyes. My skinny toes weren't touching anything. I wasn't flying. I wasn't standing. I couldn't figure what I was doing. I never did anything without standing or flying. I then heard Skeeter in a panic.

"Do you think he's dead, Mom?"

DEAD? DEAD? I thought. I must be dreaming. Now, for sure, I'll end up being a Rueben sandwich. Wait. If I'm dead, I wouldn't be hearing Skeeter and his mom.

"Rueben?" Skeeter called my name.

I felt his hands under me. I opened my eyes. I was spread out on my back on the kitchen floor. My wings straight out to my sides, I hurt all over.

Skeeter gathered up something off the floor. "He's lost some feathers."

"That's not the half of it. Look at that screen." Mrs. Whitmel was angry.

That doesn't sound good. I looked at the door and saw the top screen. It was stretched, ripped, and shredded.

"I can put a new screen in, Mom. Help me with Rueben, please."

I concentrated on catching my breath. Skeeter and his mother tried, the best they could, to comfort me. I wouldn't know how to help a winded crow either, especially one who just busted through metal screen at twenty miles per hour.

"Let's give him some water," his mother said.

Oh no. They'll try their darnedest to drown me. I clenched my beak shut. She poured the water over my beak, my face, and all down the front of me. I felt my beak open forcing air out. "Cack, cack." Winded or not, I had to get up or they'd kill me with first aid. I did not want to be a candidate for mouth-to-beak respiration. And, I knew I couldn't survive 'crow-di-o' resuscitation.

His mom aimed a glass of water at me again.

"Stop pourin' water on him." Skeeter lifted me, right side up. I gathered up my wings and managed to tuck them in place at each side. I wobbled slightly, but felt myself standing.

"He's standin'." Mrs. Whitmel said.

"He's a tough old bird." Skeeter said.

His mother pressed her hands to each side of her mouth. "Land o' Goshen"

"What, Mom?"

"The doctor called."

"How'd he know Rueben got hurt?" Skeeter laughed.

"No, Silly."

Skeeter stood. "About Jill? Did he find her?"

"Yes, he found her and he examined her, too."

"And?"

"Just as we thought, she got blood poisoning. Septicemia is the medical term. Her father got her to the hospital before she could go into septic shock."

Chapter 23

"Will she be OK? I mean normal and all?"

The mom put her hands on Skeeter's shoulders. "She'll be fine. Dr. Griffith said she'd be in the hospital for a few more days. Then, her father and brothers will be bringing her back home."

"Phew. Great. I was really worried."

"We all were, Son. Why don't you write her a 'get well' note? I got the mailing address from the doctor. We're gonna have to keep the kitchen door closed 'til you get that screen replaced.

"Yes ma'am."

The good news about Jill took my mind off my sore body. I walked around the kitchen a little bit. I did it without limping.

Skeeter closed the door and picked up more crow feathers. "Let's go, boy. You can rest while I write ole Jill-o a letter." Skeeter picked me up and cradled me next to his boney chest.

I liked being in Skeeter's room. I wiggled between his two pillows and tried not to think about my poor body blowing a hole in the screen door. Skeeter's room smelled like him. It was Skeeter's own personal scent. He has a small brown glass bottle with knobby raised letters that holds something he calls "foo foo" water. It has a sweet aroma, but not like his mother's perfume at all. He splashes some on his hands and rubs it on his face after he takes a bath. Remember, he wore it to the cotillion? This ritual is practiced only before church socials and special occasions when his father takes them all out to eat at a fancy restaurant. The truth is Skeeter just smells like Skeeter. Now that I was in the safety of Skeeter's bed, I could take a nap. And, I could sleep with both eyes closed. That's a rare treat, Bud, indeed. I drifted off occasionally while Skeeter worked.

"Look, Rueben. I'll use the stationary I got for Christmas. See?" I was not interested. I'd rather nap. Skeeter sat down at his desk, took the paper and put it on top of a comic book to cushion it from the hard wood desk. After he printed his address and the date he wrote in his best cursive.

Dear Jill, my brother,

Dr. Griffith called to say he visited with you and that you are going to be OK. I got really scared when I went to your house and you were gone. I found your diary that you forgot. I did something bad. Me and Rueben read it hoping there would be a clue where you were. I only read the last two pages and nothing else. I guess we will not be going to see Gene Vincent, the greatest Rock'n' Roller ever. I will have to use the money I saved to buy a screen for the door Rueben busted a few minutes ago. Oh, the tickets cost more than we saved anyway. But, it's OK. You will be too weak to go and I don't want to go with anybody else anyway.

Your Blood Brother,

Skeeter   (Skeeter sketched a drop of blood and colored it with red water color.)

P.S.   Rueben says, "Hurry and get well." Here are the feathers he lost while flying through the screen.

187

P.P.S.   I am prepared to take my punishment
for getting you to cut yourself. Everyone blames me.

LW

He folded the page exactly as he was taught in school and slid it into the envelope. He took a small tin box out of his desk drawer. It was the drawer where he kept important stuff. The box held a few stamps he got from the post office. After licking the flap and the stamp, he pressed his hand down hard until they were glued in place.

"FIRE!" I thought. I smelled smoke. My eyes opened wide with fright. I pushed my wings out. I was being held down. Wait a minute. I thought. I wasn't being held. It was just Skeeter's pillows wedged against me. I remembered. But, I still smelled smoke.

That boy. What's he going to do next, set his bed on fire? With me in it?

Skeeter held a red stick that had a wick like a candle. He had struck a match with a quick stroke of his hand against the rough side of the match box. The tip exploded and sent up the smoke that filled my nose holes.

"This is sealing wax, Boy. Jill will see the seal and know no one has opened the letter before she does."

I watched Skeeter tip the wax stick so the wick melted the wax, red of course. One, two, three, and then three more drops landed on the point of the envelope flap. Skeeter blew out the flame, set the wax down, and picked up a piece of shiny brass. It looked like a chess piece and was about the same size.

Working quickly, before the wax hardened, he pressed the largest side of the brass piece into the hot wax. He held it there until the wax cooled, then lifted it off. It left an impression of a capital "W" in the wax. "Perfect." Skeeter said out loud. "You stay here and rest. I'm going to the post office."

I tried to rest, but it was summer. I had all winter to rest while Skeeter would be in school. There was no way I was going to be cooped up inside.

I was sore when I got to the post office on Randolph. I stood on the roof and worked hard to catch my breath. Outside the doors of the post office, there was a big wooden pole that supported the electrical and telephone wires that served the people of Cape Charles. Not only did the pole support the wires, but it also was the place where the local funeral homes posted the funerals scheduled for the week. I watched Skeeter glance at it from the granite steps, then stop, turn around, and walk back down to its base. Each of the four paper cards listed the deceased and the date and time of each funeral. Skeeter's eyes moved across each one. With his search complete, he turned toward the post office steps, raised his face to the sky, and blew out a sigh of relief.

"That was close. I had to make sure Jill's name wasn't up there." He said softly.

He climbed the six steps, pushed on the big brass handle, and disappeared inside.

CHAPTER 24

"Skeet head!" Jill yelled when she saw him.

They were nearly two blocks apart. Skeeter ran toward her then slowed to a regular walk. He was trying his best not to look stupid. Then, he started to run again. He was too excited about seeing his friend to worry if he looked stupid. Jill started running too. When they faced each other, Skeeter smiled and mumbled out an awkward, "Hi."

Jill jumped up and down in front of him. "Hi."

They stood there grinning at each other while I flew around in circles. I was as happy at Jill's homecoming as anyone. Now we could have fun again.

Skeeter stuck out his right hand as if to shake hands with her.

"I won't break, Whitmel. I'm all well." Jill glanced at me as if I could somehow signal Skeeter that he should welcome her with a hug.

I tried with all my might to send the boy a mental signal. Hug her. Hug her, boy. She nearly died. I'd expect you to hug Peanut or Wenus or anybody who nearly died. Anybody who nearly died needs a hug. I cacked and cawed but little Gene junior didn't get it. I walked over and stood next to Skeeter and looked up at him. I pecked at his shoe until he looked down at me.

"What are you doin'?" He said.

I spread my wings and walked toward Jill. I stood between her feet and rubbed my wings against her ankles.

Chapter 24

"Careful," I heard him say. "Jill's gonna' kick the crap out of you."

Jill stood still and smiled at me. "You huggin' me, Rueben? At least you'll give me a hug."

She bent down, I pulled my wings in, and she stroked my back and head.

"Thank you," she whispered. Jill then welcomed herself home by grabbing Skeeter's extended hand, pulling it hard, and clipping him behind his knee with her foot. This caused him to hit the ground with a muffled thud. Through a cloud of dust that grew around him, he saw her shadow boxing like a fighter before a match. "I said I'm all well."

Skeeter stood up and brushed the dirt off his clothes. He couldn't get mad at her. She was just like normal. "Whatcha wanna' do?" he asked.

Jill pushed him toward Peach Street. "First, I have a surprise. Come to my house."

They took off along Tazewell. "Ah, *Peach* Street. Such a sweet street to live on, fruity too." Skeeter teased her.

"You'd better be nice."

"Since when did you care 'bout bein' nice." Skeeter held his fists up like a boxer.

"Maybe 'cause I prayed a lot to get better."

"Oh. Yea. I guess so." He said

"I'm so glad to be home."

Skeeter struggled to say something nice. "I missed you. It was so borin' with nothin' to do. Then, when we found out where you were, we just worried all the time."

"Thanks for the letter. Thank you, too, Rueben for the feathers. Stay here. I'll be right back."

Skeeter sat on the edge of Jill's porch with his feet on the ground. It was the same porch, a couple of weeks ago, where he felt so scared. Everything seemed right again. Skeeter watched me walk around the edge of the school yard in the grass next to Jill's house.

Jill let the door slam behind her, happy to be able to make noise, not like in the hospital. She sat down beside Skeeter and fumbled with some paper envelope. "Close your eyes."

I walked closer so I could see what it was.

"OK. Look."

Skeeter opened his eyes and focused them on two cards she held out to him.

"We got tickets to see Gene." Jill jumped up and down again as Skeeter stared at them.

"You're kidding. I can't believe it. Where'd you get 'em?"

"When I got your get well letter, my doctor was in the room. I told him that Gene Vincent was my best friend's idol. I told him that we wouldn't be able to go to see him. Then, he told me that his wife had extra tickets that she had bought for her friends and then they couldn't go, or wouldn't go, or somehow one lady's husband wouldn't let her go, but then the other lady said she…"

"Hold on, will you? You're talkin' too fast for me to keep up. Jeez."

"Sorry, Mr. Can't Understand English. I mean, Brother Jackass."

"Cack, cack." I laughed.

I thought I should break this up. I suppose my cacking sounded like laughter to them because they started laughing like crazy humans often do.

"Crazy Human Beans," as Mr. Floyd, the man who raised me, would say.

Mr. Floyd. I thought. I'd better get home and eat or he'll think I 'flew the coop' and there'll be no food there tomorrow. I headed home to eat a feast of cracked corn.

"Where's he goin'?" Jill said.

"You probably ran him away by talkin' so fast."

Jill wrinkled her nose and raised her upper lip. "Hardy, har, har."

"Anyway, that's so cool you got the tickets." Skeeter didn't say anything else. There was a long pause.

"Yea." Jill said, looking at the tickets.

Skeeter broke the spell she was in. "Well?"

"Well. What?" Jill raised her shoulders and held her palms up.

"Well, who are you gonna' give the other ticket to?"

"You, nit wit. Who else would I give it to? I said when I showed 'em to you that 'we' got tickets."

"Wow. Thanks."

Jill shook her head at him and pressed her lips together.

"So, what happened to you anyway?" Skeeter moved up further on the porch and leaned against the house. He stretched his legs straight out.

Once Jill started telling her story, I knew they'd be there awhile.

CHAPTER 25

After my snack I took off to join the kids. They were still on Jill's porch. Jill had made cookies from a recipe her mom had. Skeeter's cheeks bulged as he chewed.

"They're so good. If you keep practicin' cookin', you'll probably be a famous cook for sure."

"Well, maybe. I copied down a bunch of recipes from the magazines they had in the hospital."

"Look." Skeeter said to her. "I'm sorry you got sick. It was all my fault. I should have never let you cut yourself. My dad's sore at me and my mom is too."

Jill arranged cookies on the plate. "Once my dad knew I was gonna' get well, he yelled at me for being stupid."

"What? What do you mean, 'once they knew you would get well'? Didn't they always know that?"

Jill spit. "No. They thought I might die for a couple o' days."

Skeeter felt sick in his stomach and so did I. He actually turned white at the thought. There was no way I was going to turn white. But, I felt sick too.

She spit again. "Well, it was my fault too. But, it turned out OK."

"As long as you're OK. I guess it did. Come on. I want to show you somethin'."

I watched the two of them in front of Jill's house. Skeeter took the basket off the front of his bike and Jill balanced on the handlebars. They took off on Tazewell. I ate the crumbs from Jill's delicious cookies.

Once I had scavenged the leftovers, I hit the sky. I flew high over Tazewell and over the houses on Monroe, then north on Fig toward the creek. My guess was right. The three of us got to Skeeter's boat about the same time.

"I have a surprise for you, now. Skeeter said to Jill. Skeeter led the way up onto the pier and out to the end. Jill looked across the water then straight down into it.

"I don't see anything." She turned around to face the shore and saw the stern of Skeeter's boat. It would never be referred to as Skeeter's boat again. On the boat's transom, Jill read the name *Spirit* painted in bright blue letters with darker blue shadowing. It was Skeeter's best cursive.

Jill covered her mouth with both hands. "I don't believe it. I can't believe it." She felt her eyes want to get watery, but fought back with all she had. She didn't want to get mushy. She spit hard at the sand.

Skeeter and I knew she'd like it.

"When you went missin', me and Rue came back here and just hung around a lot. I scrubbed and sanded the burn marks out of the bottom. I was scared you were already a spirit."

This was painful. I watched Skeeter. He looked over at me. It was all we could do not to cry too. "I don't know what I'd do if I lost my best friend." We stood in silence, not able to look at each other.

Jill got us out of it. "Hey, Piss Ant! Let's get this *Spirit* boat movin'. I need a bushel of crabs to cook up for supper."

"Cack, cack." I agreed.

Skeeter shoved off. *Spirit* skimmed along Kings Creek then out into the great Chesapeake Bay. "You wanna hear something funny? Skeeter asked her.

"Sure."

"OK. Well, once a week in fifth grade we had a time after lunch when each kid could get up in front of the class and tell a story or show somethin' they brought from home or somethin'. One day, Wenus raises his hand to go up, and Old Lady Hedgepeth said he could. So me and Shad and almost everybody else start smiling 'cause Wenus would never do this before."

"Where was Peanut?"

"He failed first grade so he's a year behind."

"He failed first grade? How do you fail first grade?" Jill stared into space in deep thought about failing first grade.

Skeeter got slightly annoyed at her distraction. "Are you listenin'?"

"Go on." She snapped out of it.

"Anyway, Wenus gets in front of the room and turns toward us. When he realized we're all lookin' at him, he just freezes."

Then Mrs. Hedgepeth said, "Herbert?"

"A minute or so goes by, then, Wenus smiles and says, 'What would you do if you had a million dollars?'"

"Well, we all just look at him and smile back, but nobody answers. Then Wenus says, 'If I had a million dollars, I'd buy a new heinie, because mine has a crack in it.'"

Jill's eyes got as big as Moon Pies and she started laughing like crazy.

"Ah, ha, ha, ha, ha, ha."

Skeeter laughed, too, as he finished the story. "Everybody just busts a gut laughin'. It didn't matter that you weren't suppose to laugh at stuff like that in school. But, nobody could help it. The whole class went into hysterics. Even Old Lady Hedgepeth was laughin'. She tried not to, but Wenus was just too dumb lookin' not to laugh at him."

"What happened next?"

Jill was laughin' hard as Skeeter told the story. I couldn't keep my beak closed either.

"Wenus just walked back and sat at his desk. After a long time, Mrs. Hedgepeth said, 'That's not an appropriate subject matter for the school classroom, Herbert.'"

"Wenus just looked down and said, 'Yes ma'am.'"

They laughed for a long time as *Spirit* skimmed across the water.

"Hey Buddy, my arm hurts. How about you rowin' awhile?"

Skeeter rested the oars in the locks and the friends traded places. I was delighted that things were back to normal. They wouldn't be for long.

CHAPTER 26

The night before the Gene show, I was napping on the Whitmel's side porch. Skeeter was dancing around the dining room, having a Gene attack, singing "Be bop a lula, she's my baby," over and over until his parents and I could barely stand it.

"Who is your baby, Skeeter?" his dad grinned as he asked the question.

"Sir?"

"Who is your baby? You keep singing, "she's my baby."

"Aw, Dad. There is no baby. I don't have any baby."

"Well, you must. You keep singing about her. I'll bet I know who she is."

"Why do you have to tease me about girls? I don't have a girl friend. I don't even talk to any girls."

"Stop teasing him." His mother said.

"Jill's a girl." His father kept on.

Skeeter's face turned red and his brow started to wrinkle above his eyes. "No, she isn't. I mean, she is but I don't think of her as a girl. She's just a friend. Same as any other friend." Skeeter jumped to his feet and stomped them on the stairs toward his room. "I hate that crap." Skeeter growled and slammed his fists into his pillow like a champion boxer finishing off his opponent. But, that was last night. This night he was finally getting to see Gene Vincent and the Blue Caps and nothing would interfere.

Chapter 26

The Whitmel family car made the trip from the ferry terminal at Little Creek toward downtown Norfolk. They had watched the sun set on the ferry ride from Cape Charles. The sky had turned into the kind of twilight in which magic happens. The wind hesitates and thinks about what kind of breathe to blow next. The moon took over the mystic sky, full as all get out. Weird stuff happens when the moon is like this. It's as if that big round face is laughing at everyone.

"I think I'll name the moon Tom Fool," Jill blurted out. "My daddy told me that folks get caught up in Tom Foolery when the moon is full and high as a Georgia pine."

"I never thought of that," Skeeter's mother said. "You two be careful in there, now. You two stay together and close by each other and don't get lost."

"Ah, Mom." Skeeter wished she would stop talking to him like he was a little kid.

Jill tried to sound ladylike. "We'll be careful, Mrs. Whitmel."

"Maybe you two should hold hands so you won't loose each other."

"Aaahhh. We're not tradin' cooties, Mom."

Jill agreed. "I don't think we have to go that far, Ma'am."

Skeeter thought all along that he would surely attract the attention of tons of good looking girls. City girls, real rock'n'roll girls who would just fall all over him. He knew he had the look. He could answer any question about the rock'n'roll bands, their music and their life styles. He wondered at some point why he was even thinking about girls. Gene was the only reason he was there.

The city burst with carnival excitement when the sun was totally asleep. Horns blew, sirens wailed, and radios blared as the rock 'n' roll pilgrims passed tons of apartment buildings along Virginia Beach Boulevard. It seemed like days since they left Cape Charles, but they were finally there. Teenagers were everywhere. Jill and Skeeter had never seen so many kids in one place.

"I don't see anybody our age," Jill said quietly.

Jeez. Why'd she have to say that? Skeeter thought to himself. He didn't want his parents to think too hard about it. Nothing would stop him from seeing Gene Vincent now. They were there. Actually, I should say, we were there. As Skeeter's family got dressed for the trip across the bay, I hoped into the family sedan. And after studying the spaces beneath the seats, I snuggled into the roomiest one. It was directly beneath Skeeter's mom. It was perfect. I could hear everything. The chances were slim that no one would wave their hands around looking for something.

Girls huddled and squealed and jumped around like they had bugs up their skirts. Big skirts with sequined poodles on them hovered like beach umbrellas above their black and white saddle shoes. Their boy friends had enough grease in their hair to lubricate every train engine and coal car that passed through the Eastern Shore for eight straight years.

Neither Jill, nor Skeeter, nor his parents had ever seen hot rods like the ones they saw that night. Even the hot rods shown in magazines were mostly black and white pictures. Candy apple red was Jill's favorite. But, Skeeter was totally lost in a purple metallic '38 Ford with chrome everywhere.

"Got your tickets?" Skeeter's dad asked.

Skeeter rotated his skinny butt off the seat and pulled out his wallet. It was a sad looking thing that his dad gave him when his dad got a new one for Christmas two years ago. It was limp, with no lining left in it and hadn't smelled like leather for years. Skeeter removed the tickets and waved them in the air.

"Yes sir."

"All right, then. Meet us right here as soon as the show is over." Mr. Whitmel had twisted around behind the big steering wheel and stretched his long arm across the back of the front seat. He had a big grin on his face as if he wished he were going to the show too.

"Thank you for bringing us here." Jill said.

"Yea, thanks," Skeeter echoed. Now git outta here, Skeeter thought to himself. He knew he shouldn't have thought it. He just couldn't wait to be a real rock'n'roller. Tonight was his to rock hard, meet girls, and to experience the ultimate show, Gene Vincent and the Blue Caps.

The building was a giant of a place to Skeeter and Jill. They'd never been inside such a place. It was actually two different places. Half was the Center Theater, a real theater with big maroon curtains across a stage and rows of fixed seats that had real upholstery. The other half was the

Norfolk Arena and was used for everything. Basketball, professional boxing matches, ice shows, everything could be seen here. That didn't matter now because tonight was about the newest sounding music in a million years. rock 'n' roll, baby.

Jill was overwhelmed with it all. "It's like being at a circus. I'm so excited, or nervous or something."

"Me, too." Skeeter said.

I managed to find an opening in the wall between the arena and the foyer large enough for me to pass through. I kept high enough in the roof framing to keep out of sight.

Skeeter's parents watched them walk toward the entrance. Jill slowed to let Skeeter pass her. She kicked the bottom of his shoe as he walked past, then laughed as he stumbled to keep from falling.

"Will you stop it for once?" Skeeter stared at her, hoping nobody saw him stumble.

"Whoa," Jill said. "I forgot Gene Junior is on his way to becoming a teen idol."

Skeeter hoped she wouldn't be annoying the whole night. "What's wrong with you? Why are you acting this way?"

"Don't be so serious. Why don't you want to have fun?" Jill put her hands on her hips, started to spit, but didn't.

Skeeter fingered the tickets in his hand. "This is serious. I'm gonna' see Gene Vincent in a little while. I've been waiting for this the whole summer. Act your age. You're a teenager aren't you?"

Jill focused on the pavement, pressed her lips together, and twitched them from left to right. Skeeter had seen her do this a millions times. Whenever she didn't know what to say, but was thinking about it, she moved her mouth around. He liked when she did it, but right now he wished she wouldn't do anything childish.

It was a good thing Jill didn't spit, because the Whitmels were watching from the parking lot. "Poor Jill." Skeeter's mom whispered.

Mr. Whitmel looked at her. "What did you say?"

"Nothing. Well, Jill's so confused. I feel so sorry for her, not having a mother. She needs a woman to teach her certain things."

"I'm sorry she doesn't have a mother, too. But, she seems all right to me. She's a tomboy, and, a good one at that."

"She'll become a young lady soon, with no one to help her."

In a fatherly tone, Skeeter's dad said. "She has a father and brothers to help her."

Skeeter's mom continued to watch as the blood brothers disappeared through the huge doors. "You don't understand."

"I guess not." Skeeter's dad said.

"They're way too young to be here. This is a mistake to bring them to a rock'n'roll show. I think we should buy tickets and keep an eye on them."

Mr. Whitmel put the car in gear and eased forward. "If Skeeter saw us in there, he'd be humiliated and never forgive us. No. We're going to a movie like we planned. There are plenty of policemen here."

"Policemen? Maybe there's a reason for them being here. Maybe they're expecting trouble." Skeeter's mom was getting herself worked up.

"Let 'em grow up. Jill can take care of herself and Skeeter too. Don't tell him I said that." Skeeter's dad was happy that Skeeter and Jill got the chance to be here.

As they got closer to the arena doors, Skeeter was trying to act his coolest, like he had seen Gene Vincent and even Elvis many times before. But he was overwhelmed. The teenagers seemed way older and bigger than they were. He felt like they could be trampled any minute and no one would ever be able to recognize their remains. Skeeter was starting to feel sick with fright.

At least Jill seems to be OK with being here. I need to get myself together, get control of myself. Suddenly, Skeeter realized that he had never been very far away from his parents or some grown-ups that he knew before. Ever. He started to panic. Where's Jill? Oh, God. She's gone. Skeeter thought. Skeeter spun around ten or twenty times looking for her. He looked like some sort of running down toy wooden top about to fall over. His stomach felt sick.

"Skeet head. Skeeter." It was Jill. She was just a few yards away near the man taking tickets. "You look sick. Are you OK?"

Skeeter watched some tough looking boys looking in their direction. "Sure. I thought you got lost, that's all."

"We're not even inside, dummy. How could I get lost?"

"Stop callin' me Skeet head."

"OK. I'm sorry. I'm just havin' fun with you."

"Let's go." Skeeter said.

They followed other kids to the doors where the yellow lights inside made the ticket takers look like silhouettes. Skeeter stuck out his hand and a man snatched the tickets from him, tore them in half, and shoved them back at him.

"Hold on to these stubs for the door prizes," the man coughed at them. Cigar smoke rolled between them, causing the man's face to glow blue.

"Where'd you get that?" Skeeter nodded toward Jill's handbag.

"Daddy gave it to me. It belonged to my grandmother and then to my mother."

It was small, had a long strap, and hung from her opposite shoulder. It was definitely a lady's bag. It had a fancy fake diamond near the top and a silver colored metal clasp. Jill thought she looked old enough to carry it. And, she did. She caught a glimpse of her reflection in a glass partition. She stared at herself awhile. She didn't look like a little girl. But she didn't look like the poodle skirt girls either. Tom Fool must be actin' up. She looked at the reflection of herself again. Still no boobs. Wish Tom Fool would git a little more foolish, she thought.

"What 'cha got in there anyway?" Skeeter interrupted her self examination.

"In where?" Jill shouted in Skeeter's direction.

Skeeter jumped back as if she were going to take him down. "In your handbag. What's with you?"

"Oh. My handbag? Sorry." Jill grabbed the bag and pushed the clasp with her thumb and peered inside. "Well, I have a clean handkerchief, a mirror, a pink plastic comb, a coin purse, you know about that, and a pack of Juicy Fruit gum. And, inside the purse are three quarters that my Daddy gave me. You want a piece of gum?"

"Sure. Thanks."

"I'm savin' my ticket stub. It's a souvenir, you know. I'll put it inside my coin purse. Don't let me forget where I put it."

"OK." Skeeter said.

The foyer of the arena was lit up real bright. Vendors in skinny white paper hats shouted out "Popcorn!" and "Candy!" Kids hurried around stuffing their faces with hot dogs and peanuts and washing it all down with colored sugar water disguised to look like fancy soda. Hot smelly air rushed to get out of the rest rooms every time someone passed through a door.

"It sure stinks, don't it?" Jill said.

"A million times worse than the boys room at school, and that's gross." Skeeter added.

Groups of boys and girls hurried by them pushing and bumping into them like they weren't there. Most of the time, they just looked at them and kept going.

"Aren't they soooo cccccuuuuttttte???" Some girl gushed in their direction. Three other girls whipped around and stared at Skeeter and Jill.

"What woods did you and your little brother come out of?" Some dumb poodle skirt wearer teased Skeeter. "Past your bed time, isn't it kiddies? Ha, ha, ha."

"Oh no," Skeeter thought. "She's gonna get us thrown out before I see Gene."

"I'm no boy." Jill stood stiff. And leaning forward, she stared Miss Poodle Skirt in the face. "Ever had a little kiddy give you a bloody nose?" Jill said calmly.

"Uh-oh." Skeeter said, and spun Jill hard to the right, grabbed her wrist and pulled her away. Jill was going with Skeeter, but she continued to stare at the girl.

"Look at that. She acts like a boy too." The girl shouted at them. "Leave them alone. Your parents wouldn't have let you come within three miles of this place when you were that age." One of the girls must have had good sense.

"I never want to be like them." Jill said. She was about to boil.

"Forget it. They're just city jerks." Skeeter told her. "Are we goin' in or not?"

"Let's go." Jill said.

Through the doors that separated the foyer from the giant hall, they stood and tried to take it all in. The stage was at the far end of the floor. The stage curtains were closed and colored lights outlined the edge of the stage. Kids were standing everywhere. There were rows of wooden folding chairs, hundreds of them. They were marked off in sections and by seat number. Skeeter remembered that their seats were in Section "L". It smelled like a gym in there. He spied a big card on a pole with "L" on it.

"Over there," he said, and they set out to get seats.

"Everything seems so big." Jill said.

Intimidated at first, Skeeter now felt like he was as big as anyone there. He felt like he belonged there, like everyone else. After all, he was finally going to see and hear his idol. Skeeter settled onto a hard oak chair. He could barely see because a behemoth of a guy was directly in front of him. Two rows in front of him was a girl who had twisted around in her seat and was smiling at him. She wouldn't stop. Skeeter wondered if he had snot on his face or something. I hope my hair looks OK, he thought.

He tried not to look at her. She made him nervous. It was the oddest thing. He was getting crazy. He wanted her to think he was cool, but, she had hard hair like the bully girl. He was getting plenty confused.

What am I thinkin'? What are you doin'? Skeeter wondered to himself.

Skeeter just sat there looking back at her smiling face. He felt a stupid grin stretch his lips across his teeth and felt the Juicy Fruit, now flavorless, slide out of his mouth and onto his pants. What was that? You idiot. He tried to keep from yelling at himself.

Mystery girl closed her left eye real slow and opened it again.

"Oh, no." Skeeter said. "She winked at me."

"What?" Jill answered.

"Nothin'." Skeeter said. "Look. The lights are goin' down."

"Did you say, 'she winked at me'? Who winked at you? A girl?"

"Yea." Skeeter felt funny inside. He and Jill had never talked about stuff like this.

"Tom Fool." Jill said. "Don't start thinkin' you're some kind of Romeo, here, Romeo. You're with your little brother, you know." A huge smile broke across her freckled face. They looked at each other and laughed, the way best friends do.

Skeeter took a gum wrapper from his pocket then rolled it into a ball. He held up his hand and took aim, closing one eye. He lobbed it over the heads of the people in the two rows in front of him. Toward the girl who winked at him, the sphere arched up and then floated down only to get caught in her hair. It clung to the hair spray and reflected light rays as the spot lights announced that something was about to happen on stage.

Jill turned toward Skeeter's face. "Why'd you do that?"

"I dunno'."

God, he's such a dip stick. Jill thought. He's a know-it-all and he thinks he's the greatest boy in Cape Charles. He's actually the biggest jerk on the planet. Jill put a stick of gum in her mouth. "Why don't you just go over there and tell her you want to marry her or somethin'?"

"What's with you? You're just jealous because nobody winked at you."

"No. And I don't care about winks, or boys or any of that crap. And, I really don't care about you. Llewellyn Whitmel. What kind of name is that anyway? You....you jackass."

"Whoa," Skeeter sneered and made a mocking face.

Jill saw what he did and without thinking stood up, spun around and bolted toward the aisle.

Skeeter didn't see her leave. He felt weak. In a split second, during Jill's hissie fit, Skeeter realized that an older looking teenager with big freckles and long red sideburns had seen him fire the tin foil bullet.

"You got somethin' to prove? Hey, Ugly. You got somethin' to prove?" He was looking right at Skeeter. "That's my sister you're messin' with. And, unless you want to carry some of your teeth home in your pocket, you ought to move somewhere else where I can't see your ugly face. Don't you even look at my sister, ya jerk."

Skeeter gulped hard and swallowed a mouthful of spit he had worked up with the Juicy Fruit.

"Sorry," Skeeter barely grunted out. It won't happen again."

He looked up slowly. Oh no. The flirting girl was all the way turned around and smiling at him again. Skeeter hadn't thought about Jill. He pointed his face toward the floor, kicked his legs into high gear, and followed the smell of greasy fries and the glimmer of yellow lights out toward the lobby. Holy crap. He thought.

Chapter 26

He ducked behind a broken down popcorn machine and tried to hide for awhile. "Great, now that's great." Skeeter's hand brushed the back of his pants and felt nasty popcorn grease smeared across him. He was feeling a little miserable.

The teenagers there seemed to get bigger and older looking too. Maybe this wasn't such a good idea to come here. Nearby, also hiding from the light, were four or five guys standing in a tight circle. At first Skeeter didn't see the winking girl's brother with them. When he did, he dropped himself straight down to the floor, squatting like a girl. He could see them laughing in a secretive sort of way. They kept moving their heads around looking to see if anyone was coming their way. They had a flat looking brown glass bottle, not round like a soda bottle. They took turns drinking from it and passing it to the next guy. Skeeter caught a whiff of the stinking stuff when one boy choked and spit on the floor. That must be whiskey. Skeeter thought. Cripes. If that girl's brother sees me now, he'll beat me to a pulp. I'm doomed to end up dead. And, Jill will have to ride home with my parents, by herself.

This is dreadful and seriously dangerous. My hopes for Skeeter and Jill to have fun are now in jeopardy. I saw Skeeter hiding from the bullies, as well as Jill walking near the girls' restroom.

Jill got boiling mad with herself for telling Skeeter to go ask the girl to marry him. You idiot, Jill. What do I care if he wants to flirt with girls anyway? No girl would want him for a boy friend. He doesn't even know about girls. Not once, ever, has he mentioned them, except to say how goofy we are.

What's Jill doing now? She saw someone leave a cigarette pack on a table that still had a cigarette in it. Don't smoke that nasty thing. I wished I could tell her. I couldn't fly down to her and take it from her like I could if we were in Cape Charles. If I expose myself in here, surely someone would take a broom to me and set off hundreds of people on a crow killing frenzy.

Jill was so upset that she felt like she had to do something bad. She saw a kid who looked like he would be OK giving her a light. She took a deep breath and in a "by-the-way" gesture said, "Can I get a light?"

The guy was watching girls walk by. He stuck his hand in his pocket and produced a Zippo. He opened the top, spun the wheel with his thumb, and held it out to Jill, all in one motion. Jill smelled the lighter fluid as the wick burst into flame. She barely touched his wrist as she leaned her head toward it. She sucked air through the cigarette until it caught fire. She drew some smoke into her lungs, exhaled it opposite the guy's face and muttered, "Thanks."

Oh, no. Now she's smoking. I'm going to work on this problem when we get home.

Skeeter stood up from behind the popcorn machine. He walked a few steps and blended into a group of kids who were moving quickly and talking like mad men. Once he got past the bullies and out in the open foyer, he saw Jill.

He walked up to her, looked her in the eyes and said, "Why were you talkin' to that guy?"

Jill tried to look tough. "He lit my cigarette. What's wrong with you? You jealous or somethin'?"

"No. And, just like you, I don't care about girls and winkin' and all that crap either." Skeeter was giving Jill her own lecture. "The difference is I do care about you. You said you didn't care about me." Skeeter grabbed Jill's hand and took the cigarette from her. He closed his lips around it. He bit the end with his teeth, sealed his lips around it and took a deep breath. The smoke burned his eyes. At the half-breath mark, he couldn't take anymore.

"Ah hack, ah hack, ah hack." Skeeter coughed and yanked the cigarette away. Smoke came out his nose, his mouth, and he felt like it was coming out his ears too.

This is terrible. Skeeter looks as if he is on fire.

Jill watched him coughing, hacking, and snorting like crazy.

Jill laughed at him. "You OK, Big Stuff?" She waited until he calmed down. "I care about you. Who else would be your blood brother?"

Skeeter didn't answer. He hacked some more and wheezed out, "That's awful."

"Let's go. The music's startin.'" Jill said as she spun him around and pushed him toward the doors.

"Ladies and gentlemen! On his first visit to Norfolk, please welcome, Carl Perkins!" The public address system boomed the announcement.

I need a rest. I hope Jill and Skeeter stay put for awhile and watch the show. All this is giving me a headache.

"What?" Skeeter stared at the opening curtains, "Where's Gene?"

"This is a new band that's playin' first." Jill read from a pamphlet she got with her ticket.

"Whoosh, whoosh." I'm still able to fly short distances up here. Everyone is watching the band. Ah, here's a spot shielded from the speakers. I can stand here and still see my friends without the danger of becoming deaf.

Everyone, including Jill, clapped their hands for Carl and the boys. Skeeter joined in though he could hardly wait for Gene. He had dreamed of this night for three months. Had he not found Jill to pass the summer with, he would have driven himself and me crazy.

Why is Skeeter staring into space with a dumb grin on his face, I wondered? He looks like a simpleton. He looks frozen.

Skeeter stared right through the Carl Perkins Band and focused on a scene he had stored in his mind. He saw himself standing in the ally where they met. He saw Jill exactly as she looked the first time he'd seen her. He imagined seeing her throw baseballs for Wenus and Peanut to hit in the outfield.

Skeeter thought about seeing Jill's blood run down her hand when they became blood brothers. He recalled the terror he felt when her dress caught fire. He felt sick again thinking about her going missing. A sharp pain in his ribs broke Skeeter's trance.

"Ohhh." He grunted as Jill pulled her elbow back to her side.

"Wake up, Skeet head." She jabbed him again.

"I'm awake."

"What 'cha thinkin' about?"

"Huh? Oh, nothin'. When's Gene comin' out?"

"Soon."

The Carl Perkins Band had cleared off the stage. Behind the curtain, the stage hands constructed the holy altar. Amplifiers and instruments were placed. Lights and sound equipment were checked.

Out front, a feeding frenzy was brewing. The arena became quite eerie. It was the oddest feeling, almost electric. That's it, Bud, there was electricity in the air. Carl Perkins' music was replaced with the excited hum of the crowd, the squeaking of chairs sliding across the floor, and the muffled chaos of the back stage shuffle. Just when the crowd couldn't wait any longer, the house lights went dim. Spot lights that seem so bright they could blister the paint from an airplane a thousand feet in the sky, passed over the crowd causing temporary blindness to those eyes caught in their paths. There were three of them bouncing above the arena's frantic rockers. The mob roared when the three became two. My eyes were big as pie plates. I wrapped my toes tightly around the steel roof brace where I was perched. Skeeter and Jill were well within my sight. They stood close to each other and shook as if the temperature had plummeted to zero. As I tried desperately to dodge the lights as they zipped by me, one changed course abruptly and my luck ran out.

"ZAP!" I was hit. I couldn't see anything but a big orange ball like the sun. I lost my balance, my muscles relaxed, and I felt out of control. I knew if I fell I couldn't recover, never glide out of it. Imagine, a crow falling upside down, meeting his death at the feet of thousands of jitterbuggers. Oh, the humiliation of dying indoors.

The multitude screamed even louder when the two spot lights became one. Finally, I got my senses. I was hanging upside down, just as I feared. Of course, I could no longer hear anything. I spied a similar roof support four feet or so below me. With all of my concentration, I let go my grip, tucked my legs up under my feathers and did a complete and perfect forward roll. I recovered by spreading my wings and floating to safety. Once I was able to focus on my friends, I felt in control again.

The solitary spotlight slowed. The stage curtain would soon part and there he would be! Skeeter was vibrating. His eyes were fixed and they could hardly contain themselves in their sockets. Jill jumped and weaved next to him trying to get the best view. The light crept along the curtains then to the ceiling and finally stopped to the left of the stage.

Right in the center of the spot light, a tall dark man got up from his chair and walked toward the stage. He grabbed a hand rail and climbed the steps to the stage and approached a waiting microphone stand. He turned to the audience, beamed the world's greatest gold toothed smile and into the microphone he announced.

"LADIES AND GENTLEMEN. PLEASE WELCOME, NORFOLK'S VERY OWN HEART BREAKER, GENE VINCENT!"

The place was deafening with cheers. Girls screamed "GGEEEENEE!!" over and over. The music began like a clap of thunder. The drums and bass guitar hammered out the beat; the guitar wailed and stung the air.

"It's Willie T!" Skeeter yelled. "It's Willie T!" Not even Jill heard him. He screamed out, "It's Willie T," a few more times and still no one heard him. No one there ever heard of Willie T, anyway. Actually it was exciting to see Willie T. I felt famous just knowing the man who introduced Gene Vincent. Willie T had once tossed me some bread crust off his sandwich.

Then, when I thought it could get no louder, Gene, himself, the almighty of rock 'n' roll appeared like white smoke out of the night. Skeeter was totally overwhelmed. He couldn't look at Gene hard enough. He was actually there. He was actually there in the same room with the man he idolized most in the whole world!

Gene Vincent and the great Blue Caps played eighteen songs. Skeeter sang along with every song, every word. He didn't care if anyone heard him. No one did.

Jill watched the spectacle as if it were her first time at a circus. After a few songs, she watched Skeeter and smiled. She was happy he finally got to see Gene.

Who is Willie T? She wondered. Why was Skeeter so excited about Willie T?

Jill glanced at Skeeter. He stood next to her in over-all shock, no longer aware of her. It was OK. She studied some girls nearby. She and Skeeter were the youngest teen-agers there. And, that was OK, too. She was proud she could stick up for herself. She felt proud of her daddy and brothers for looking after her. They couldn't help it that her momma died. They didn't know about girl and woman stuff, but still managed to watch after her.

Skeeter broke out of his trance. "You havin' fun?" He smiled at her.

"Hell yea. You?"

"Hell yea."

At the height of the excitement, Gene sang the final song, said good night, and left the stage.

It was over.

The house lights came up. The magical, mystical, rock'n' roll spectacle had vanished. "Come on." Skeeter took off for the stage.

They wove their way through the kids heading out. "Watch out kid." Some big guy barked at Skeeter. "What are you doin', jerk?" Another one said.

Skeeter plowed ahead with Jill in his path.

"Where we goin'?" Jill asked him.

"First, maybe Gene's still here and I can talk to him. Maybe, get his autograph. And, second, I gotta' talk to Willie T."

"Who's Willie T?"

"The janitor at school. You know him. Oh, that's right. You haven't been to school yet. He's the man who introduced Gene." Skeeter reminded her.

"You know him?" Jill said. "He looked familiar."

"Hell yea. We've been friends forever. I need to know how he got here and how or why he introduced Gene."

They passed some girls sitting on the floor crying and saying "Gene" this and "Gene" that. Jill kicked a couple of popcorn boxes out of her way. Hot dog wrappers, napkins, stomped relish, flattened onions, puddles of water and garbage like I had never seen, littered the floor.

Willie T appeared from a door marked Men's Locker Room just as they neared the stage.

"Tell the truth!" Skeeter called.

"And may the Lord love ya." said Willie.

For the first time ever, Willie T and Skeeter didn't shake hands when they met. Skeeter nearly knocked Willie T to the floor as they hugged each other. Willie T nearly knocked Skeeter over. But, it was from the stench of the funeral home suit. Skeeter's eyes squeezed shut when he caught a whiff of it. It didn't matter. He was overwhelmed with excitement. They held on to each other, rocked around from side to side, and jumped up and down.

Jill laughed too and joined in the hug. Not for long, though. The wool fabric of Willie T's suit coat irritated her cheek. But worse, the odor of it caused her to ditch the hug as fast as she had joined in.

Pheeww, she thought. Somethin' stinks.

The other two continued with the festive dance, unaware of her joining in and of her abrupt departure.

"Why didn't you tell me you were going to do this? How did you ever get to introduce Gene Vincent? Is he still here? Please let me meet him! Please!"

"Hold on. Hold on. First, he already done left to catch a bus to the next show. He ain't here."

"But, how'd you get here? I mean how, did you come to introduce Gene?"

Because Skeeter was convinced Gene had gone and that he had no chance of actually meeting him, he and Jill concentrated on Willie T's story. Willie explained how he had spent several days visiting an injured cousin who was hospitalized in the Naval Hospital in Portsmouth. During his visits with his cousin, he met Gene who was recovering from his motorcycle accident. Willie told his young audience that back then Gene wasn't famous and he went by his real name, which was Vince Craddock.

"Vincent Eugene Craddock is his real name." Skeeter added to Willie T's story.

Jill was proud of Skeeter's knowledge. She felt like she was a personal friend of Gene's as she listened.

Chapter 26

"As it happened there in the hospital," Willie T went on, I was one of the few people who thought Gene's music was good. I praised him and gave him encouragement, when all his Navy buddies walked away."

"But, please, how did you get to introduce him?"

"As it seems, a few days ago Gene ran into my cousin from years ago. And, when my cousin told Gene that I still lived nearby, somebody from Gene's show left a message for me telling me that Gene was sendin' a car to pick me up and get me to Norfolk for this night. My, my, what a time I had. Yes, Lawd."

"Lucky." Skeeter proclaimed.

"Yea. Lucky." Jill added her endorsement.

"I say, all y'all's pretty lucky too. You got to see Gene Vincent and the Blue Caps. And, you got to see Willie T introduce 'em on the big stage too. Lawd have mercy."

"Oh, no." Skeeter said. "I'm sorry you two. Willie, this is my friend Jill. She's the new girl who moved to town. She's the one I asked you about at the cotillion."

Willie T faced Jill and bowed slightly. "I sure am proud to meet you ma'am?"

"Thank you. It's good to meet you, too." Jill used her best manners. She didn't mention that Willie T had shooed her away from the back doors of the gym that night.

"Oh, Lawd. I almost forgot sumthin'." Willie T reached under the steps he'd climbed to introduce Gene. He gripped the tattered leather handle of a well traveled cardboard suitcase and pulled it into view. The snaps popped open and Willie T produced a big brown envelope and handed it to Skeeter. Jill blinked her eyes as the stage lights from above reflected off Willie T's gold toothed smile.

"Go 'head boy. Open it."

Skeeter's eyes were nearly as big as Willie T's. He fingered the contents of the envelope and slid the papers out. Sandwiched between two pieces of cardboard for protection, was a real photo of the great Gene Vincent and the Blue Caps.

"Holy Moly." Skeeter studied it like he'd only get this one chance.

Written right across the left corner of the picture it said. "To Skeeter. I'm happy you got to see the show. My best to you. Gene Vincent"

"Holy Moly. I can't believe it." Skeeter read it over and over.

"Can I touch it?" Jill asked.

"Be careful. Don't tear it."

Jill wanted to say some smart Alec remark and throw him down. Nah. She thought. The boy's just excited.

"Thanks, Willie. Thanks a million."

"Y'all git now. Your father be waitin'. I'll see you soon at the school."

Willie T watched them join the rock 'n' rollers making their way to the exits. He rubbed his hand across his lower jaw. "Lawd. My face hurts from smilin' so much. Ha, ha, ha. Oh, Lawd."

Jill looked back over her shoulder and saw Willie T massage his jaw. When Willie bent over to grab his suitcase

Chapter 26

she stopped for a second and faced him. "Tell the truth." She shouted in his direction.

Willie T barely heard her but he could read her lips say the word 'truth.' With his bag in his left hand, he held up his right and with the slightest wave, said, "And, may the Lawd love you, chile."

CHAPTER 27

Skeeter held his most prized possession as tightly as he could without bending it. He was in a trance and didn't speak for quite a while. Then the flood gates opened. Skeeter opened his mouth and talked and talked, non stop. Jill listened, rubbed the scar in her hand, and tried to add something to his observations. She couldn't. He kept on. People crowded around the exits and the pace slowed. They stopped walking. Talking like a mad man, he waved his hands at her as if to bring back the image of the grand rocker on stage. Skeeter's dream had come true.

Soon, the crowd moved again and they made their way toward the lobby doors. The magic of the night, the lights, the music, the whole rock'n'roll experience were the thrill of Skeeter's lifetime. And the fact that his best friend was with him made it even better. But, something else happened that neither of them would ever forget.

As the crowd moved closer together to get through the doors, the back of Skeeter's hand barely brushed against the back of Jill's. For a millisecond, Skeeter felt a wave of confusion. And, similar to an electric shock, his hand automatically jerked away. He pushed his fingers into the palm of his hand and massaged his scar. He pretended to accidentally touch her hand again. This time he held his hand against hers as long as he could without Jill being aware of it. His heart beat loudly. It was hard for him to breathe.

All summer, they'd thrown each other to the ground a thousand times. They'd pulled splinters out of each other's hands and feet. They had bandaged each other's cuts and scraped skin. And, until this instant, he'd never given it a second thought. Never.

Without thinking, Skeeter stuck his hand in Jill's direction like he was groping around in a dark basement. When the back of his hand touched hers the third time, he slid his hand inside of hers. For a second, he was afraid of what she would do. What if she pushes me away in front of all these kids? What if she throws me down? What if she laughs at me, or screams, 'what are you doin'? Skeeter's heart thumped like Gene's drummer pounding the bass.

Skeeter held her hand. He held his breath too, and imagined her worst reaction. When he realized she was holding on to his hand too, he exhaled without making a sound. Without looking at her, Skeeter walked faster.

A half step behind him, and with a wide eyed look on her tanned face, Jill held on and followed her best friend. Before they got to the lobby doors, Skeeter saw a tall set of collapsed bleachers pushed out of the way of the exit. He aimed the two of them in that direction.

Once they had ducked into the shadow of the bleachers, he turned to face her. Still holding hands and now face to face he said, "This is the best summer of my life. And you made it that way."

Jill felt a confused smile stretch across her grape soda stained lips. She saw Skeeter's teeth as he smiled back. She looked totally different from the Jill he'd seen all summer. Skeeter let go of her hand. Reflections from the colored stage lights moved across her face. The colors were the same as those that lit their faces the night *Spirit* caught fire. Skeeter was just as scared now as he was that night.

Then, Skeeter stopped smiling. Jill looked up at him and stopped smiling too.

Oh no. I gasped at the thought. What is happening?

Skeeter leaned his head toward hers. He moved his face closer and hoped his lips would touch hers. Jill couldn't look. She just froze. When he believed his aim was perfect, Skeeter kissed her mouth. Skeeter kissed the mouth of his best friend.

What am I doin'? It feels nice, I guess. I'm too scared to feel anything. Skeeter's mind spun around in confused circles. Skeeter smelled grape soda and Juicy Fruit gum on her soft lips and Aqua Velva and Old Spice on her skin. Nothing ever smelled better.

When Jill felt Skeeter's lips against hers, the sound of her heart beating nearly deafened her. She didn't know what to do. She pressed her lips together and kissed him too. What's he doin'? What am I doin'? I feel so weird. She felt dizzy, too.

At what Skeeter thought was the appropriate time, he backed away. He looked at her and said, "This is the best day of my life."

For the first time in her life, especially since she'd met Skeeter, Jill said nothing. She made no wise cracks, no sarcastic remarks, no challenges, and no playful insults.

"Holy crap. Did you see that?" Jill and Skeeter heard a girl's voice.

"I've never been kissed like that." Another girl sighed.

"You've never been kissed at all." said a third.

They stared into each other's eyes until Jill reached out and hugged her arms around him. They hugged each other tightly, not caring if anybody saw them. Jill put her mouth close to Skeeter's ear. "Thank you for making me feel like a real girl for the first time in my life."

Skeeter held on. "I think you're the best girl and the prettiest girl ever."

For the first time since moving to Cape Charles, Jill could hold back her emotions no more. Squeezing Skeeter so he'd never leave, she felt tears flowing from her eyes. She buried her face in his shoulder. Skeeter smelled delicious, the same as the night of the Cotillion. She rubbed her face against his shirt, hoping the tears would go away. She opened her eyes and saw three poodle skirts looking at her.

"What does she have that we don't? No boobs and she gets kissed like that."

Look here, Bud. I wish I hadn't heard that.

Jill squeezed her eyes shut and hoped 'the teen idol' hadn't heard it either. Without speaking, they moved away from the bleachers and rejoined the crowd in the slow procession to the lobby. They passed through the lobby and through the doors to the outside. The first car they saw was Skeeter's parents'. Without thinking about it, they let go of each other's hand and raced each other to the car. Before they could tell any story about their adventure, they saw Skeeter's dad standing by the rear door.

"Look inside." He told them.

Skeeter opened the rear door and saw me standing on the back seat of the rock 'n' roll Chevy.

"Rueben. How'd you get here, boy?"

"Holy Crow." Jill said.

Skeeter stepped inside the car and slid across the seat toward me with Jill behind him. Skeeter reached out to pick me up, but I stuck my right wing out to keep him in the center of the seat. I looked him directly in the eyes and stared. He stared back at me and smiled slightly.

"Rueben won't move over," Skeeter said to everyone.

"That's OK." Jill whispered.

Skeeter and Jill told his parents all about the Gene Vincent show. They told about the kids they saw, the food they ate and music they heard. They laughed when Skeeter told about seeing Willie T. My beak was sore for the next two days from smiling so much.

During the ride home to Cape Charles and through all of the excited stories and the laughter, only the three of us knew that Skeeter and Jill never stopped holding hands.

ABOUT THE AUTHOR

Bruce Brinkley was born in Virginia. He graduated from Princess Anne High School in Virginia Beach, Montgomery College in Rockville, Maryland, and from Old Dominion University in Norfolk. He has written articles about fire protection, American antiques, and blues music. He currently lives with his wife on the Eastern Shore of Virginia.